To Beverly

Lots of love

Martin X.

Maurice Minor's Incredible Adventure

A Children's Book for Grown-Ups

by
Martin Forey

authorHOUSE®

AuthorHouse™ UK Ltd.
500 Avebury Boulevard
Central Milton Keynes, MK9 2BE
www.authorhouse.co.uk
Phone: 08001974150

First published by AuthorHouse 1/21/2010

ISBN: 978-1-4490-6875-2 (sc)

Acknowledgements:

I won't lie to you, most of the work involved in the creation of this book was entirely my own, although there are still a few thank-you's to be made. I would like to thank Bex for her assistance with all IT related aspects of its development and her tolerating my (frequent) outbursts when these didn't run smoothly. Thank you to Lee 'The Captain' Kirk for helping out with reformatting some of the illustrations and Mark for allowing me access to the office at weekends and use of work stationery. Mustn't forget little Chloe for her excellent efforts with an alternative cover which will hopefully still be used on a later edition. I would also like to thank all those friends and family who have read various early drafts and given such constructive, faith-fuelling feedback. But most of all, I would like to thank and apologise to the family of mice who, in being forcibly evicted from their home behind my washing machine, provided the inspiration for this story.

For Mr Davis

Although based on actual events, all the characters referred to in this book, with the exception of maybe one or two, are purely fictitious. Any semblance to any real animals or humans, or combination of the two, whether living or otherwise, is purely coincidental.

The origin of the name 'Battenberg' is not clear but one theory claims that the cake was created in honour of the marriage, in 1884, of Queen Victoria's granddaughter to Prince Louis of Battenberg; Battenberg being a town in modern Germany. The four squares of the cake are said to represent the four Battenberg princes.

Wikipedia (on-line) 2007

Maurice

As the little mouse lay there, stirring, listening to the shrill calls from his mother to hurry up and get ready, he beamed a broad, toothy smile. Such cheerful mood at this unearthly hour of a new term Monday morning was rare among mice of his age; but then, Maurice wasn't like most other mice. He didn't share the same distaste for school that was the accepted norm among his peers; in fact, quite the contrary; he fair cherished every moment that he spent there. He loved learning; his mind a tiny sponge, greedily soaking up all manner of facts and figures across a whole range of subjects. His hunger for knowledge was indiscriminate and knew no bounds.

Forty five minutes later and a freshly groomed and buffed Maurice arrived at the gates to his beloved Eton Mouse Elementary School for the Moderately Gifted (and those with sufficiently wealthy and proportionately generous parents). He stood for a moment, taking in the scholastic scene with his usual corresponding levels of excitement and trepidation, for school, although offering potentially boundless wisdom and wonder, was not without its hurdles to a mouse of his particular stature. The playground and surrounding fields were a hive of running, jumping, scurrying activity; the collective murmur of huddled group conversations recounting the exaggerated adventures entered into over the school holidays, carried to him on the morning breeze.

Over to his left, two first years were playing conkers with seed-pods suspended on miniscule lengths of cotton. One was berating his scornful adversary for an earlier defeat, claiming that he had quite obviously soaked his weapon in vinegar and baked it in the sun prior to combat, thereby rendering his victory obsolete and the score-card wiped clean, yet again. This was not the first time that Maurice had witnessed this whole scenario being acted out between these two and he felt quite sure that it wouldn't be the last. Four female mice, possibly from the third year, although Maurice couldn't be sure (they were certainly much older than him anyway), played at skipping using an elastic band which was just perfect for their purpose; mice were extremely resourceful in this way. Two leapt up and down in unison in the middle, whilst the 'twirlers' at the ends sang gleefully (and also in unison) in time with the twirls and jumps: 'E-dam, Che-ddar, Gorgon-Zola'. As he scanned the crowds, Maurice's eyes finally (and with no mild sense of relief) alighted upon what he'd been searching for all along, picking out the comically mismatched figures of his only friends; Tiny, Slim and Podge. Their real names were Tony, James and Roger but, since their appearance in the story is only fleeting, we won't go into laboriously detailed and unnecessary explanations as to how they acquired these nicknames, although the more educated reader will hopefully be able to picture the scene and take a stab at a reasonably accurate guess.

As he worked his way through the throng of furry bodies and came a little closer, his steps slowed as he realised that the inevitable dreaded morning ritual was already in full swing. The resident gang of school bullies, The Back Breakers (they had a fearsome reputation and the name was a reference to the dreaded steel-sprung human traps which had claimed so many an unsuspecting victim) were shoving his friends from one to another, jeering insults, calling them the usual uninventive names and insisting, quite forcefully, that they hand over any food that they might have on them or be prepared to suffer the consequences. As was his want and rather than turn and flee (which would still have been an easy thing to do at this point since his presence had not yet been fully acknowledged by any of the group), Maurice took a deep breath and soldiered on into the battle zone. His turn would come soon enough and now was as good a time as any. He might just as well get it over with; not that it would ever be completely over, you understand – and as Maurice himself also understood all too well. As he neared, Tiny was the first to spot him. He glanced over at his approaching friend and some of the fear ebbed from his stricken face, replaced by a little rouge to the cheeks as some blood returned. The gang's ring-leader, Gripper, must have picked up on this, subconsciously or otherwise, because he turned immediately to face this new addition to his morning fodder.

"Oh my" sneered Gripper "and look what we have here! Just when you thought they couldn't make them any nerdier, along comes a new and improved weedy little geek!" His comrades laughed heartily. Even Maurice himself had to admit that this was surprisingly imaginative abuse for the usually neanderthal Gripper and, in an uncharacteristic instant of reckless bravado, he told him so. Tiny, Slim and Podge all gasped as one. Although suppressedly so, they were mightily impressed and proud that one of their own group could ever do such a thing and stand up to the ghastly Gripper but didn't dare let their faces show it, for fear of the obvious repercussions. Maurice wouldn't always be with them when the Back Breakers were around. Gripper's eyes narrowed, brow creased, his nose wrinkling and face filling with even more hatred than was his trademark. He took a step forward, moving toward a resignation-filled Maurice.

"*What* did you say, *Cat* Food?" This was the most derogatory title that one juvenile mouse could ever bestow upon another and was usually a signal that they intended to make mince-meat out of them, although could also be used occassionally in light-hearted banter among friends; it was really all in the delivery. The more cunning mice would often expand on the theme to insult others without them realising it and there was much accolade that accompanied the clever and successful abuse of another unsuspecting recipient, particularly when the insultee was larger and stronger than the insulter; the more daring, therefore, the better. There was one arrogant, show-off bully in the fourth year, for example, who had been nicknamed 'Whiskas' during his first term at school and had embraced and proudly carried the self-ridiculing pseudonym ever since. He naively believed it to be in recognition of the superior length and impressive rigidity of his follicular facial appendages, the envy of the whole school (since this is what he had, by all concerned, been deliberately mis-led to believe) when it was, in fact, a play on the common Cat Food cuss. He was just too full of his own thick-skinned self importance and general all round brilliance to suspect anything else. Another female mouse in Maurice's own tutor group was nicknamed Sheba, because of, or so she was told, her regal presence and generally striking resemblance in any number of ways to the Queen of Sheba (they had covered the topic in Human

5

History class). She quite obliviously added further insult to her own self-inflicted injuries by confirming that, yes, it was funny that they should say that because she did indeed have some Royal ancestry a little way off, in the not too distant past; much to the uncontrollable mirth of all those around her.

Gripper's delivery on this occassion, however, was anything but light-hearted. The way that he spat out the word '*Cat*' with sinister emphasis made his intentions only too clear. Maurice stood fast, silent, a wild look of fear and determination in his watery eyes. Gripper took another step forward.

"Leave it Grip!" warned one of his goons "Remember who his brothers are!"

"How could anyone ever forget?" snarled his leader's disgusted response "Damn do-gooders!"

"Yeah, but are you going to tell them to their faces?"

It was a rhetorical question. They all knew the answer to that one. Maurice's older brothers were captains of literally every school sports team, excelling at all physical activities; it was widely acknowledged by anyone who knew them that a virtually guaranteed, glittering military career stretched out ahead of them in the RAF (Rodent Armed Forces). They were resented for it by many jealous individuals but none had so far had the courage to challenge their unrivalled status as the Big Cheeses, the

Alpha-mouse twins of the upper school. Paradoxically, their undisputed supremacy and his sibling status only served to highlight and exaggerate Maurice's physical inadequacies so that he was verbally ridiculed and picked on but ultimately left unharmed by the bullies in equal measures.

The school bell chimed. This was a first warning that lessons would be underway in just five minutes.

"Saved by the bell, *Cat* Food!" Gripper repeated his venomous delivery of the phrase and sloped away, vowing that this wouldn't be the last that Maurice would hear of this, oh no, and that he'd better keep a low profile and stay out of his way from now on if he knew what was good for him, you could count on that, yes sir, and his brothers wouldn't be at the school forever, and so on and so forth. He knew though that he too had had a lucky escape. The other Back Breakers hurried after him, not themselves without a similar sense of more than mild inner relief also. If Gripper had overstepped the mark and actually struck the little fellow, they knew that they too would be guilty of the assault by association and didn't much fancy the idea of tackling the vigilante twins, out to avenge their little brother.

As the second bell chimed and the Head-Mouster patrolled the school perimeter, the grounds cleared as the mice filed in with varying degrees of urgency and haste, depending on their enthusiasm for the next lesson on their particular timetable. Those who had PE, or any other of the less academic subjects, would usually be the first in from outside, keen to get ready to go back out onto the school field; whereas Maurice could invariably be seen at this time, shuffling dejectedly along, dreading the inevitable pitch persecution from both the staff and his frustrated, despairing team members alike. Conversely, whenever Maths, Literature, Geography or Science was on the menu, Maurice would be first in the classroom, waiting eagerly at his desk in the front row for the results of last night's homework, often before even the teacher himself had arrived. Perhaps obviously to an outsider, this didn't help to endear him to any but a small minority few like-minded individuals (namely Tiny, Slim and Podge) who had now forged a close friendship through their mutual social rejection.

Maurice checked his new timetable and his heart sank as he saw that first session was indeed games. He wouldn't be so cheerful on Monday mornings from now on, not for the rest of this term at least.

Out on the field and just a brief ten minute stint at team ball sports later and Maurice had already been substituted. He was grateful for the early reprieve. His Games-Mouster, Mr Fitz, persevered with him unerringly and tried to include Maurice as much as possible in a vain attempt to involve him and improve his skills and although the little mouse knew that the teacher's intentions were good, he sometimes wished that he wouldn't try *quite* so hard. They both knew that he was never going to make any of the school teams in a million years and so his heart just wasn't in it. His passion and talents clearly lay somewhere else entirely; with his mastery of pen control and tackling the written word.

Sitting at the sidelines, Maurice watched in admiration as the other fine physical specimens from his year hurled themselves headlong into every challenge, sprinting majestically down the wings after the Subbuteo ball with powerful hearts pumping and heads seemingly free of the inferiorities that he was burdened with daily, and wished that he too could fit in and be more like one of them. His mind wandered to daydreams of alternative, very different Maurices that he might otherwise have been. There was Cool Maurice; 'Double M' they would call him and they'd all hang on his every word, waiting for him to throw them some paltry scrap of kindness, a sign from their chosen one that meant that, just maybe, they had the slimmest chance of being accepted into his fold; a charming grin, a cheeky wink, the tiniest nod of agreement would be all that was needed to make their day, their week, their very existence and he'd dish them out in meagre doses to make them all the more coveted and ensure their value. Then there was Maurice the Adventurer, successfully returned from yet another epic journey of exploration out in the big wide world; the all conquering hero, astounding all who came from far and wide to hear the stories of his encounters with fearsome foes as they paraded him atop their shoulders to riotous chants from the adoring, waving crowds lining the streets;

"MAU-RICE! MAU-RICE! MAU-RICE!"

"Maurice!" came the agitated shout from Mr Fitz, breaking Maurice from his fanciful, wishful thinking. "For goodness sake boy, are you completely deaf? Why, I must have called your name a dozen times or more!"

"Sorry Sir, I ......" Maurice wasn't really sure how to explain.

"Yes, well, never mind being sorry!" interjected the Games-Mouster, as ever favouring promptness of action over the need for a lengthy and most likely uninteresting, drawn out explanation. "Session's over, you'll no doubt be pleased to hear. Time to hit the showers. Not that you really need one, I don't suppose, after that decidedly mediocre effort, I'm sure."

Maurice ventured to apologise again but thought better of it, instead rushing off to do as he was told, with a sudden slight spring in his step as he took a quick look at his crumpled timetable. It was Algebra next!

The Major

Major Maurice was a very proud mouse. A very proud mouse indeed. Probably the proudest in all his regiment. In fact, apart from the day that his two eldest sons, the twins Robin and Barry, were born, the day that he enlisted in the Mousehold Guards was easily the proudest moment in his life. More so, even, than the day that he got married and definitely more so, although he would never openly admit it, than the day that his youngest, Maurice Junior (it wasn't until years later, in the Mouse School playground, that he would become affectionately known as Maurice Minor due to his diminutive stature and 'Maurice Major' for a father), was born – a blind and hairless little pinky.

His wife, Mary, always accused him of using up all his love and affection on his first two children so that he had none left for poor little Maurice. He, of course, said that this simply wasn't true and instead accused his youngest of being a mummy's mouse. 'You give him more than enough love and affection for the both of us' he would say. But the fact was that Maurice Minor was simply not enough of a true housemouse, like his brothers were, that his father had hoped that he too would be. 'We are Mus Musculus', the Major would bark, referring to their proper Latin name, 'Not Mus Minimus!'. He didn't like the fact that little Maurice wasn't interested in sports, preferred reading and had his own ideas about what he wanted to do in life. He accused him of lacking discipline, saying that he should join Mouse Cadets, like his brothers, to learn how to look after himself and build up his feeble little frame with a bit of proper hard training and exercise, just as he himself had done as a youngster.

As a carry over from his army days, The Major was also obsessed with maintaining immaculate personal presentation, hygiene and grooming. He knew that he couldn't get his sons to line up for parade inspection, as he secretly wanted them to, as this would cause arguments with Mary who already accused him of being overly militaristic and trying to force his excessive rules on others. Instead, he did the next best thing and developed a strict regime of dental hygiene every evening before bed-time. All three brothers would be made to brush their teeth for at least five full minutes until they were gleaming white and then stand with their backs pressed firmly against the bathroom wall, mouths fixed in a grimmacing wide-open grin, so that their father could march backwards and forwards in front of them, fore-paws clasped firmly behind his back, nose pointed skyward, sniffing the air, with his whiskers bristling. The whole family was well known in the area for their magnificent pearly whites.

Little Maurice though, was often made to return to the sink for at least two more minutes of frantic brushing, supposedly because his teeth were not as dazzlingly white as his brothers. 'Beige!' Would be his father's usual exclamation. Little Maurice really couldn't see any difference himself on the frequent occassions when this happened but his father always muttered under his breath, complaining that it was his son's expressly forbidden, almost bordering on obsessive love of Battenberg cake which was causing the problem. It was indeed true that, such was his love of the marzipan covered sponge delicacy, a number of classmates had nicknamed him Lord Mountbatten. Maurice wasn't quite sure what it all meant but he liked the attention and the idea of being a Lord, nonetheless. 'Cake means sugar, means decay!' The Major would rant, trying to drum the message home to little Maurice. It didn't go unnoticed by Maurice, or his mother for that matter, that he only ever seemed to be punished in this way when he had been caught with Battenberg though. If Maurice so much as mentioned Battenberg, or 'a nice bit of Batty' as he would sometimes refer to it, The Major would go into a blind rage. Countless times he had been caught by his father, nibbling away on a nice piece of Almond Slice or Lemon Drizzle Cake, without it seeming to be any issue at all. Maurice wondered if it might actually be something to do with the Battenberg being pink. Once before, he remembered, his father hadn't approved when one of his older brothers, Robin, went to a fancy dress party and had worn luminous pink socks as part of his punk outfit. The Major had flushed red in the cheeks and made him go to his room and change before leaving the house, claiming that the socks would be too easily spotted by cats, foxes and the like. Maurice took some small comfort in the fact that his father was probably therefore only worried for his safety. Maybe the Battenberg could also be easily seen by dangerous predators as he strolled along, obliviously tucking into it. He couldn't help thinking that this was being unnecessarily cautious though. Ok, so the first rule of mouse-school was always to stay out of view, but his father must be colour blind if he thought that Battenberg was as bright and visible as those gaudy, flourescent pink socks! He very likely wasn't really worried about tooth decay at all, Maurice had always suspected. Something about the way that he said it just didn't add up. His father was obviously not a very good liar but at least that mean't that he loved him, just as he did the twins....didn't it?

Maurice lay back, contented by his own thoughts, and pondered to himself, for the first time, how quiet and uneventful it had been outside for the last few days. It dawned on him that it might even be safe enough now to venture beyond the curfew zone that his father had set out for the family in their new home, and go exploring.

Tom

Tom waved goodbye as his father pulled away in his beaten up old Mercedes estate. He chuckled inwardly to himself and wondered affectionately if dad would ever get around to buying that brand new Turbo Diesel that he'd been looking at in the brochures and promising himself for what seemed like an eternity. The salesmen at the local showroom probably rushed to take their break now when they saw him coming along again, misting up their nice clean windows with his nose pressed up against the plate glass, trying to summon up the courage to spend some of his hard-earned savings. It wasn't as if he couldn't afford it.

He'd only been away visiting an old travelling buddy for a long weekend but Tom always liked to get back to his own beachside flat, make a nice cup of tea and put his feet up in front of the television to unwind before going back to work again the following morning. The journey home had been unusually arduous. Although usually a flight of less than an hour, a lubricant leak under the aeroplane had meant a long wait, sitting on the runway at Jersey until an engineer could be rushed out to have a look. As it turned out, the whole thing had been caused by just a single loose nut. Tom thought how he would rather have his flight delayed by a single nut loose on the ground than find out that there was one in the cabin once they'd taken off. His initial exasperation at the news of the delay had been quickly soothed by his comfort in the knowledge of all the rigid security and safety precautions which had now become such an everyday part of flying. The captain had previously announced over the tannoy that they might have needed to change planes if the problem had been anything more serious, so Tom again thanked heaven for small mercies and looked on the bright side as ever. A change of planes would certainly have taken a whole lot longer and caused more inconvenience than staying comfortably in his seat and reading his book. Even the horrendous bank holiday motorway traffic jams on the final stretch at the other end coming home had failed to completely dampen his spirits. In all honesty, after a weekend of partying with friends, he was probably quite simply too tired to get annoyed about anything, and he was glad dad had driven, even if it was at a slow crawl, so that he could close his eyes and listen to the pop charts playing softly on the radio.

Tom watched his father disappear around the corner, then breathed a sigh of relief as he hoisted his bag back onto his shoulder and put his key in the front door.

His relief was short-lived however. As Tom rounded the bannister at the top of the stairs, into the hallway, he was met with a strong and not particularly pleasant smell. Usually he was quite fastidious and unusually domesticated for a bachelor living alone. In fact many of his friends and colleagues would mock him, telling him that he was bordering on obsessive-compulsive. His mum regularly claimed that he was 'set in his ways' and worried that he had been living alone for far too long and would find it increasingly difficult to settle down with a nice young lady and provide her with the grandchildren that she so desperately craved. So this was unusual. Tom had only booked his flight to Jersey at the last minute and had not had time to carry out his usual pre-trip cleaning rituals. From experience, he usually remembered, before leaving, how nice and relaxing it was after having been away, to come home to everything looking spotless and smelling pine-fresh so would bleach, disinfect and polish every visible exposed surface, making sure that not a single item of crockery or cutlery was left unscoured out on the sideboard. On the day of departure, he had made lunch and called a cab to take him to his parents but the car had arrived unexpectedly early and so he didn't have time to wash up after eating. Amidst all the rush, he had only just had a few spare moments to scrape a few scraps into an opened black rubbish sack on the floor and leave the dishes for when he returned. It shouldn't really matter too much; or so he had thought at the time. He was only going to be gone for a couple of days, after all.

The problem though, was that he had eaten salmon fillets that day and left the skins and the plastic supermarket container in the rubbish sack without tying the top.

The overpowering piscine odour filled the room. Tom put his bag down onto the hallway floor and walked into the kitchen, which was separated from the lounge merely by a breakfast bar in an open-plan living arrangement. He knew immediately that he would still not yet get the chance to reacquaint himself with his much-loved sofa until he had cleaned and freshened up the room and so set about running some piping hot water into the sink and adding a healthy squirt of 'fruits of the forest' scented washing-up liquid. Tom wished at that moment that he wasn't so environmentally opposed to using aerosol sprays and that he had some air-freshener somewhere in the cupboard under the sink. After just having taken two flights in only the last three days, he reckoned that he might have been able to live with the guilt of using the comparitively insignificant household spray, particularly given the severity of his plight; his quest for stink-freedom and untainted lazy repose on the beckoning settee. He could always walk to work the next morning, rather than take the car, in an effort to offset the guilt of polluting the atomsphere. He did his bit; he didn't leave the video on stand-by, he didn't leave the tap running whilst cleaning his teeth, he deliberated, before realising that all these attempts at convincing himself were unnecessary since he didn't have any air-freshener anyway!

An industrious half an hour later and the bin liner was double-tied, put outside and replaced with a new one; gleaming washing-up dripped white foam suds onto the draining board, the kitchen worktops shone like fragrant mirrors and the opened sash windows welcomed in a light breeze, swapping the warm, stale, pungence for cool, fresh summer evening air – and an exhausted Tom finally felt that he was ready to make a cup of tea and go and sit down with his treasured remote control. He flicked on the kettle switch, dropped a tea-bag into his new 'I Love Jersey' (the word 'Love' was represented by a red heart shape) souvenir mug and rummaged around in the cupboard looking to see if he could track down some biscuits, lurking somewhere behind the five year old gravy granules and sachets of also-past-their-sell-by-date blancmange mix. He really should clean these cupboards out when he got the chance, he thought - but not tonight.

There were no biscuits to be found anywhere but he did manage to find a few things of interest which he hadn't even been aware were there before. He certainly hadn't purchased them himself. A couple of weeks previously, Tom had gone to the local park with friends to spend the day eating and drinking in the sun whilst listening to the annual Royal Philharmonic Orchestra open-air performance. One of the highlights of his annual social calendar, this had been something of a growing tradition which had steadily become a bigger event each year, with the guys all bringing drink and the girls bringing the food. As he lived the nearest and taxis were virtually impossible to come by on this particular night, what with all the thousands of revellers leaving the park at once, everybody in his party had invariably ended up back at Tom's flat, carrying on the festivities into the early hours - much to the delight of his neighbours, he was sure. The mess in his lounge the following morning had always been partly compensated for by the quantity of left-over food and drink in his fridge and cupboards for the next few months. Something of a rarity, he knew all too well, in an otherwise typically empty bachelor pad.

As the electric kettle bubbled then billowed clous of steam and switched itself off, whistling its satisfaction at another job well done, Tom reached for the sugar bowl and managed to find something sweet to go with his hot drink - an unopened box of mini-Battenberg party cakes.

Tea

Tom put the Battenberg onto a small side plate, squished the last bit of flavour out of the tea bag, threw it into the newly started bin-liner – he really should get a proper pedal bin soon – and went and sat down in front of the television. As the screen crackled to life, blue light flickered and darted around the room, bathing Tom in an atmospheric glow as he bit into his cake and took a cautious first sip of his scalding tea to wash it down with, blowing on it first in a rather futile attempt to cool it a little. He'd never tried Battenberg before and it was a lot sweeter than he'd realised. Sugar stuck around his lips and he instinctively licked them clean, doing the same with his now slightly sticky fingers too. If he'd known beforehand, he might have put a little less sugar in his drink. The combination of sweet tea and marzipan was a little too sickly for his more savoury taste-buds and so, after another tentative bite, just to make sure, Tom grudgingly lifted himself out of his seat, walked around the other side of the breakfast bar and dropped the rest of the cake into the rubbish bag with the still steaming tea-bag, before resuming his place on the sofa. He knew that if he hadn't done this right away, he would undoubtedly have ended up falling asleep right there and then, in front of the telly, just like he always did; and didn't really fancy the idea of waking up to find a dropped plate of battenberg squashed into the furniture, and most likely his clothes too. He was right to be careful. Within less than five mintes he was asleep, twitching to surreal dreams of swimming underwater in his flat, which had inexplicably turned into a giant aquarium, filled with huge exotic fish, as his tea cooled down, slowly developing a mottled film on the breakfast bar behind him.

The Dream

Tom managed to swim to the surface, coughing and spluttering, gasping for air in an effort to relieve his aching lungs and reach for a high open window a couple of feet above the water line. As he used all of his remaining strength to pull himself out of the water, giant fish toothlessly sucking and nibbling at his toes, he squeezed his dripping torso through the tiny space and clambered down onto an outside window ledge, looking out over the Jurassic world below. What he saw took away what little breath he had just mustered; From his vantage point, it seemed to Tom that every living thing had been magnified to at least ten times it's usual size; with starlings the size of pteradactyls swooping across the sky and beetles as big as dogs scurrying to and fro, going about their business in the usual urgent, purposeful way that they do. Tom felt extremely exposed, high up here on the outside of the building, and knew that he needed to find a way down as soon as possible if he was to stay out of danger and take stock of his situation. He looked first to the left and then to the right but the wall below was a tall sheer face with no drainpipes or other ledges on which to climb. He looked straight down and noticed, to his immense relief, a huge pile of swept leaves and compost directly beneath him, built up against the wall. There was nothing else for it. He would have to take his chances, jump and hope that they would be deep and soft enough to cushion his fall. There wasn't even much opportunity to summon up the necessary courage to make his move. A flash of yellow and black in his peripheral vision and a sound similar to the blades of a nearby helicopter, as the wind from a giant approaching wasp's vibrating wings ruffled his hair, was all the encouragement that he needed and Tom leapt for his life.

Time seemed to slow down as he fell through the air; so much so that he was acutely aware of every stone in the pebble-dashed wall flashing gently past him as he tumbled to the ground like an astronaut, suspended for a moment in a miniature space odyssey. But gravity got him in the end and Tom plunged like an apple from a tree, disappearing into the mound of rotten garden debris below.

As he lay there, too scared to even try moving for a minute, for fear of what breakages or other injuries he might discover, Tom realised with joy and new-found bravery that he had miraculously survived the drop relatively unscathed, save for a few small surface scratches, and so set about climbing out of the second of his unusual surroundings that day. As he crawled to the surface, sweeping the last few feet of dry, dead, rustling leaves aside, he found his was out into the daylight once more - and out of his dream.

The Discovery

Tom's eyelids unstuck themselves and he glanced blearily around the room, realising, with ever such minor irritation, that he'd done it again. Why didn't he ever just go and get into bed straight away and watch TV on the small portable in his bedroom so that he could remain where he was until the morning if he fell asleep? He chuckled to himself, knowing that he would probably never learn. Now he had the unwelcome ordeal of having to trudge up the stairs, clean his teeth, get undressed and climb into a cold bed, all the while attempting to maintain a state of half sleep so that he didn't wake fully and would therefore be able to more easily drift off again back to slumberland as soon as possible. As he lay there on the sofa, taking advantage of the luxury of time to summon up the energy to move that he hadn't had when standing on the window ledge in his dream, Tom thought that he heard a sound. A rustling sound maybe? Maybe leaves in the wind outside? The window was open after all. He reached silently for the remote control, slowly eased the television volume down and sat forward to listen, newly heightened senses awake and on full alert all of a sudden. There it was again. Definitely not leaves. No, he was increasingly certain that it was coming from the kitchen, behind the breakfast bar. It was the new rubbish bag that he'd put down on the floor earlier. Maybe it was just moving as some of the things that he'd put in it fell off of each other naturally? But no, he was pretty sure that there was some life behind the movement. It was too erratic to be merely a milk carton sliding to the floor and he hadn't yet put much in the sack anyway, other than a piece of cake and a tea bag. Tom discretely lifted himself out of his sunken position on the settee, taking care to make as little sound as possible, and crept quietly out to the kitchen, placing his feet down ever so gently so as to avoid creaking the floorboards and disturbing his mystery guest.

He could clearly see the crumpled bin-liner moving with a life all of it's own and knew immediately, without question, that there must be something inside. Although that something would clearly have to be pretty small, fear of the unknown made his heart race and for a second he paused, hesitantly, before deciding that it wasn't really likely to be anything that he should have cause to be afraid of. There was no real dangerous wildlife in England that he was aware of, other than perhaps the venomous adder and he couldn't see it being a very realistic likelihood that a snake could have found its way up to his first floor flat - or ever wanted to for that matter. As thoughts rushed through his head, eliminating unlikely possible candidates, he concluded quite quickly that it was most probably a....

MOUSE!

Tom had moved noiselessly until now but the shifting weight of his body had caused a barely detectable movement of the wooden floor underneath the carpet, alerting Maurice to the fact that his unwitting host must have finally woken and was almost upon him. He rushed out from the cover of black plastic and paused momentarily, unsure of the safest route back to his family. Pausing similarly, with eyes locking on Maurice's for the briefest of moments, a startled Tom stood open-mouthed in disbelief as he watched the tiny little grey-brown figure scurry across the floor, holding a sizeable chunk of pink and yellow Battenberg cake almost half its own size, and disappear behind the washing machine.

The Trap

The following morning and Tom stood brushing his teeth in front of the mirror, getting ready for work, shaking his head in disappointment at the rather weary looking reflection staring back at him as minty lather dripped down his chin. Last night hadn't allowed him the hours of unwinding that he'd been so looking forward to, following his journey back from the Channel Islands. What with all the fraught cleaning and then the unsettling discovery that he had a mouse in the house, Tom had barely managed half an hour on the sofa before being woken from his traumatic dream by the rustling in the kitchen. When he had finally managed to get to bed, he'd lain awake for hours, staring at the shadows on the ceiling, wondering what to do about it the next day and intermittently flicking his head from left to right, imagining that he had seen some small movement out of the corner of his eye. Every sound, every creak caused by the cooling night, he'd imagined to be a mouse. He had to move fast, he worried to himself, before that one mouse turned into lots more mice. Obviously he didn't realise that the rest of Maurice's family were already living beneath the skirting boards, behind his washing machine.

Once dressed and fuelled full of breakfast cereal, Tom took the time that he'd set aside, by getting up slightly earlier than usual, to go into his study and switch on his computer. After about only ten minutes of research on the internet, he'd learnt that you could buy humane traps which would catch mice alive, rather than the traditional, old-fashioned spine snapping versions that he had so often deliberately set off with a stick as a child when he'd discovered them in his father's shed, by the old rabbit hutch. He also discovered that, once caught, mice should be taken at least a couple of miles away from where they were found to avoid the possibility of them finding their way back again. Despite his eagerness to remove the mouse from his flat, Tom couldn't help but be impressed by this. How on earth did they know how to navigate their return? It wasn't as if they could read road signs. Tom knew what a complete and utter lack of any sense of direction he himself had. If it hadn't been for the satellite navigation equipment in his car that girlfriend Pam had once bought him as a birthday present, he might very well have gotten lost just two miles from home himself!

Tom left the house and drove the short distance to the local high street where he knew that there was a discount store which always seemed to be positively brimming over with all manner of unusual household items. Despite the relatively early hour, he was pleasantly surprised to find it already open; piles of cheap plastic buckets, brooms and storage boxes spilling out onto the pavement to attract the attention of passing trade, keen to bag a very cheap but often equally unnecessary bargain. He parked right outside the forecourt, walked in and asked the attendant if by any chance they supplied mouse-traps. Without saying a word, or even so much as glancing up from his morning paper, the old man behind the counter pointed towards a display at the back of the shop and Tom set off in the direction of his gnarly, outstretched finger.

Originally not optimistic about his chances of finding what he was looking for without an extensive bit of searching, Tom was somewhat taken aback and even, in places, horrified by the broad-ranging selection available. Laid out on the shelf before him, was a whole array of different products targeted solely at catching, repelling or killing various forms of life. There were ultrasonic plug-in devices which emitted a sound inaudible to humans but disturbing to animals, deadly spring-traps, flea-powder, rat poison, fly-spray, even ultra-sticky sheets of card designed to have mice walk on them and get their feet stuck fast so that they couldn't escape. Tom dreaded to think how the poor things were supposed to be removed by their captor from this barbaric mammalian fly-paper. That was assuming that they hadn't already died of fright first.

Finally, he came across what he had set out for: the 'Rodent Rid 2000'. A surprisingly simple creation, the RR2000 (as the shopkeeper's assistant rather worryingly and over-enthusiastically referred to it – with all the salivating gusto that you might expect of a main dealer car salesman, talking about a Millenium model Rolls Royce) was simply a squaresided plastic tube in the shape of an opened out, uneven, very shallow sided letter V, closed at one end with a hinged door at the other. The idea was that the tube be placed down on the ground with the sides with the door attached remaining flat to the ground and left open, with the other, closed and baited end effectively therefore raised slightly in the air. When the inquisitive mouse entered the chamber and passed the pivotal halfway point, the excess weight would tip the trap forward, closing the door at the other end behind it. Simple.

Tom paid the elderly gentleman at the till (although, to be perfectly honest, thought that 'gentleman' was maybe rather too generous a description, since the ignoramus continued to read his paper, still didn't utter so much as a single syllable, only glancing upwards momentarily to inspect the price on the luminous orange sticky label before holding out his hand for the money and then placing the change flat down on the counter) and returned home, checking the glowing digital clock readout on his dashboard to make sure that he wasn't going to be late for work. He still had time to nip back home and set it up so that he could concentrate on other things when he got to the office, more comfortable in the knowledge that he would have done all that he could, for now at least, to resolve the problem.

Parking his car on the yellow lines outside his front door, he knew that he would have to move quickly to escape a ticket from the ever increasingly vigilant flow of predatory traffic wardens who seemed to roam the streets these days in packs. Tom fleetingly thought how much better things might be if there were as many police officers out walking the beat in the same way but his digressing thoughts soon returned to the job in hand. He ripped open the plastic see-through packaging from around the trap and looked in the fridge for something to use as bait, but it was empty as usual. Tom wondered what would possess any mouse in his right mind to want to come and set up home in a place with such little food ever available and then it dawned on him for the first time that maybe the strong fish smell from the weekend might have attracted it. He was pretty sure that mice didn't eat fish, especially since his ten minutes of research that morning had rendered him something of a mouse expert, but thought that the overpowering odour might have given animals for miles around the impression that there was a lot of unsealed food to be found here. How wrong could they be! If that really was the case, he thanked his lucky stars that he hadn't come home to a house full of cats. He knew that they liked fish because Pams' cat absolutely loved tinned tuna but supposed that they probably wouldn't have been able to find the same way in that this mouse had anyway, wherever that was.

Then the idea struck him. Why hadn't he thought of it sooner? The mouse obviously liked Battenberg. In fact, judging by the size of the piece that it had carried off last night, even when fearing for its' own safety, it was probably quite safe to say that it absolutely *loved* it. It was Battenberg that had lured the mouse out to the black sack in the first place, so it should therefore be quite effective as bait for the trap; especially as he would be out all morning and the little fellow might feel brave enough to come out exploring again whilst all was quiet. Marvelling at his own ingenuity, Tom re-opened the cardboard packet of mini-Battenbergs and broke a piece of one off, making sure to measure out a healthy enough portion to prove sufficiently enticing but not too heavy so as to close the trap by itself. He dropped it into the little black plastic tube and set it down on the tiles by the gap next to the washing machine. How could any sweet-toothed little mouse, with a clear and proven penchant for Battenberg, ever resist *that*? Tom thought confidently as he set off for work.

Gotcha!

Maurice woke up, scratched, stretched, yawned widely, looked around and listened carefully to determine whether or not any of his family were still at home. They had all gone out without waking him. This was highly unusual. Normally, The Major was vehemently against lie-ins of any kind and would rigidly insist on having everyone up in the morning at the stroke of six but when Maurice had returned home last night, looking deathly pale and trembling all over as a result of his secret close encounter, out beyond the curfew zone, his mother had assumed that he must be coming down with something and had fussed around him something awful, touching his forehead anxiously, checking for a fever and making sure that he was tucked up warm and snug in bed. His father had, of course, shown little sympathy, barking instead in his usual macho way that it was probably all her fault in the first place for wrapping him up in cotton wool. This wasn't only meant as a figure of speech either. It was indeed true that, in the past, when he'd exhibited even the slightest hint of a sniffle, Mary had been known to actually swaddle little Maurice in balls of cotton wool that she'd found in the cupboard under the bathroom sink in a previous house that they'd inhabited. 'He's not like the rest of you lads' Mary would say, referring to her husband and the twins 'he's sensitive and caring, and there's nothing wrong with that. We're all made of different stuff and that's what makes the world go around. It would be a boring world if we were all the same. You could take a leaf out of his book and be a bit more caring sometimes'. She often said the same things, or at least something very similar along those lines, but then it seemed to her that she was having to defend her youngest more and more these days as time went on and his young age became less and less of an excuse for his delicate ways. Maurice would often get up and hide around the corner, listening to his parents squabbling over him long after he was supposed to have been wrapped up snug and asleep in bed. When she got to the point of the argument where she realised that she wasn't going to get anywhere, his mother almost always ended her defence with the same proud punchline; 'He may not want to join Mouse Cadets, but he's still my little soldier!'. Maurice would cringe at this catchphrase though. He knew she meant well and that she was only trying to stick up for him but he couldn't help feeling that his mother's comments were only making matters worse. The more that she took his side, the more of a 'mummy's mouse' The Major thought he was.

When he'd only narrowly made it home last night by the skin of his excessively brushed teeth, Maurice had been too afraid of his father's anger and disapproval to admit what had really happened and confess that he'd been out exploring beyond the agreed safety limits of the washing machine. In truth, he'd also been incredibly shaken up by his narrow escape and was so relieved to get back in one piece that, for once, he'd welcomed his mothers lavish, if somewhat misguided, attentions with open paws. When he lay in bed later on however, listening to The Major criticising him to Mary for his sickliness, he had considered telling all. Maybe his father would finally be proud of him and realise that he wasn't such a coward or weakling after all. This might be just the chance that he'd been waiting for to finally gain The Major's acceptance. He wasn't ill in the slightest. He had ventured further than either of his brothers had ever dared. What's more, he had gone out on his own when the lounge wasn't even empty of people, using only the blaring din from the TV as his cover. Surely his father couldn't fail to be impressed by the considerable risk factor which that would involve? But the more he thought about it, the more Maurice realised that this might not be such a good idea after all. The first rule of Mouse School was, as he knew only too well, to stay out of view and he had most definitely not done that. In fact, they'd looked each other right in the eyes, their host and he, albeit very briefly. Dad would be absolutely furious if he thought that Maurice had attracted unwanted attention to HQ and compromised their position there. They would likely end up having to up sticks and move yet again, due to his carelessness, thereby only serving to further compound The Major's existing opinion that Maurice lacked discipline and had his head in the clouds. After careful deliberation, he thought it perhaps wiser instead to say nothing. The washing machine hadn't been dragged out from under the kitchen work surface like it had the last time that he'd been seen, at the previous house. Maybe that would be the last that he'd hear of this particular episode and everything would just revert seamlessly back to normal. Maybe.

Maurice jumped out of bed and got ready for the day ahead, starting with the obligatory five minutes of teeth brushing. Even though The Major wasn't there, watching over him right now, he still found it hard to break the habit which had been so robotically conditioned into him every morning and evening for so many months; although at least he didn't have to return to the bathroom for the extra two minutes that his father usually insisted upon, even though he'd had a midnight feast of his beloved Batty only hours before. He brushed the crumbs from the bed so as not to be found out by his dad at daily inspection later on and thought how much the colourful cake was like Chinese food. No matter how much of it he ate late at night, he always woke up feeling hungry for more.

He wondered where the rest of the family had gone off to and, once ready, thought about leaving the house to look for them, before deciding to first climb up from beneath the floorboards to go and take a peek at the washing machine, just to satisfy himself that all was well, and above board, so to speak; that it was still in the same place and that there was nothing to worry about after what had happened last night.

When he got there he saw, to his relief, that it didn't appear to have moved at all. Or was it a little further forward than normal? Maurice wondered if maybe his mind was playing tricks on him. He knew that if you looked at a freshly hung picture, it always appeared to be slightly wonky and that no matter how many times you adjusted it, it always seemed to stay crooked until you finally gave in and checked it with a spirit level just to be sure. He thought that the same thing was probably happening here; because he suspected that there was a chance that it might have moved, it appeared as though it actually had, even though in truth it probably hadn't. Before frustration set in, an idea occurred to Maurice. He didn't have a spirit-level but knew, from memory, that the kitchen appliances were all positioned neatly in line with each other and that the dish-washer was perfectly flush with it's neighbouring washing machine. All he had to do was walk down the gap between the sides of the cupboard units and the washing machine, poke his head out and look right along the length of the two appliances to check for any suspicious misalignment. Simple. No risk. He would be able to stay safely out of view the whole time. Plus, it was day-time too and generally, during most of the afternoon, it seemed to be quiet out there until much later when the TV came on again beyond the breakfast bar. Without further hesitation, he made his way along the shadowy alleyway, towards the tall thin rectangle of light at the opening to the kitchen.

As he neared his destination, he was momentarily unsettled by the sight an unfamiliar object. He continued walking towards it, sniffing the air, slightly apprehensive but, at the same time, irresistibly curious and distracted by the increasingly strong, hypnotically sweet, heady aroma of his favourite cake, drawing him in like a paper clip to a magnet. The container on the floor ahead, just a short distance further than he had originally intended to go, looked harmless enough but Maurice knew that he would still need to check it out. As he drew level with the corner of the washing machine, he first stuck to his original plan and, squinting one eye closed, cast his open eye down the line to the corner of the dish-washer. What he saw put his mind at rest immediately. The two domestic appliances were placed so millimetre-perfect, side by side, that it was hard to tell where one ended and the next began. This was all the confirmation Maurice needed that his earlier concerns had been unfounded and, with renewed reckless abandon, he strolled out to the plastic chamber to take a closer look. His eyes were drawn instantly to the writing along the side. Much to The Major's barely concealed disapproval, Maurice had opted for trying to learn to read in favour of the sports and other more physical activities that his father had tried to force upon him. He was already highly proficient in Mouse Literature and poetry in particular (he was in the top set at school) but had only recently begun learning to squeak English as one of his options. In spite of this, he relished any opportunity to put what little he had learned thus far into practice. He didn't dare venture too far from the haven of the washing-machine gap though and so tried to read what he could from the spot where he stood. He could just make out a few symbols which he recognised separately as letters and numbers, pleasantly surprised by his own ability to distinguish between the two, before finally making out 'dent-Rid 2000'. He recalled seeing something like this before when they'd lived in the cupboard beneath a bathroom sink (that was the first time that Mary had discovered the cotton wool which she had later used to wrap a poorly Maurice). He definitely remembered there being similar lettering on a plastic tube of toothpaste. Yes, that was it: it was all coming flooding back to him now. 'Dent-Aid'. Only one digit in it. His father had needed all the strength that he and the twins could muster to help him remove the screw-top lid so that he could get at the precious green and white striped spearmint-flavoured substance within, which he prized so dearly for their daily dental routine. This black plastic chamber was obviously some kind of toothpaste dispenser. Even more unbelieveably, could it possibly be Battenberg-flavoured toothpaste? Maybe pink and yellow striped? Or perhaps it was a special type of medically developed Battenberg which was good for your teeth? Either way, his father would be thrilled with his find and, for the first time ever, Maurice could finally actually enjoy keeping his teeth sparkling white. This was just too exciting a prospect for Maurice to resist and, without a moment's further pause for thought, he darted into the open entrance, rocking the trap foward in an instant and engulfing himself in darkness as the door swung shut behind him.

Solitary

Maurice froze, motionless just like a tiny Wade Whimsey, trying not to make a sound as he waited for his eyes to adjust to the sudden darkness and for the floating, green blobs to disappear from his vision. But it didn't happen. Or maybe it had happened already but the walls of the tiny box which he sat in were plain black and so gave the impression of complete lightless shadow all around. Either way, he looked down and realised that he couldn't even see his own trembling paws stretched out in front of him. He waited for something to happen, some sound from outside which might give some indication of his imminent fate but all was as motionless and quiet as it had been before he found himself stuck here. Not that he was even certain of that for a while. At first all he could hear was the seemingly deafening sound of his own panicking gasps of breath and thumping heartbeat. In the darkness, everything was exaggerated. His head was filled with the pounding, rapid rush of blood and adrenaline coursing through his veins until he feared that they might burst under the pressure. He worried too that the noise might also be loud enough for others to hear and draw unwanted attention to himself from his captor or other possible predators outside who would soon take advantage of his vulnerable predicament. But this didn't happen either. He felt so sick with terror that he had completely lost his appetite too. If somebody had told Maurice, when he woke up that morning, that he would find himself, later that day, enclosed in a small private hideaway, out of reach of his father's ever prying eyes, with a hearty helping of his favourite soft pink and yellow sponge and smooth sugary icing without being even vaguely tempted to take a bite, he would never have believed them in a million years.

Eventually little Maurice tried to look for a way out but it wasn't long before he'd explored, fumbling blindly in every direction, without success - or at least he thought he had. He wasn't so sure now. It was so pitch dark and he'd turned around so many times that he'd completely lost his bearings. He would either trip over the chunk of Battenberg, walk into a wall or up a small slope which, as he put his full, though not altogether significant, weight on it, would see-saw downwards as it had when he'd first entered the chamber, panicking him again so that he would clamber back to where he'd just come from, only for the same thing to happen all over again – the trap appearing to dance and twitch on the ground like a giant rectangular jumping bean. When, finally, he plucked up enough courage to continue on in one direction, ignoring the rocking ground, he still ended up banging his nose against yet another black wall – it just took a few more steps to get there, that was all. His little pink twitching nose was becoming increasingly tender at all these head on collisions until he decided that it was just too painful and not getting him anywhere anyway. He decided instead to remain perfectly still, as quiet as the proverbial mouse, and wait for help - or worse - to arrive.

As more minutes of nothing happening turned into hours though, Maurice's terror at what was to come subsided and the throbbing sound of his own pulse in his ears gradually relented, giving way to the comfortingly familiar sound of distant traffic. He tried to use this to guess what time it was and roughly how long he'd been in his self-inflicted solitary confinement, listening to the muffled ebb and flow of cars and motorbikes slowly dieing off as early evening turned into late night and then, finally, to the deathly calm of early morning, only occassionally broken by the faint swooshing sound of rubber on twilit tarmac.

Maurice managed to keep this up for some time but the effect was like counting sheep and despite his constant efforts to rub his eyes and remain vigilant and awake, he finally gave in to the blackness, curled up exhausted on the floor of his plastic cell and drifted off, muttering in a half sleep about how he should have listened to his father and been more careful. As his consciousness closed in on him like the end of a Warners Brothers' cartoon, his last waking thoughts were that Battenberg might just end up being bad for his health after all.

Freedom

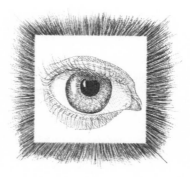

Tom had stayed over at Pam's place the night before, having gone round there straight from the office, and didn't arrive home until early the following morning. Despite being in his standard, fraught rush to get ready for work, running late as usual, the first thing that he did on entering the hallway was to head straight for the kitchen to see if the RR2000 had lived up to its package's bold claim of: 'Got a pest? By far the best. Forget the rest!' To his delight and relief, he saw that the trap was indeed closed and was hopeful that he would therefore have no need to ever consider the rest in the first place, let alone remember them again at a later date. Keen to make absolutely sure that he'd been successful though, he picked it up carefully to check that the door hadn't merely swung shut by itself and at first wasn't sure if it had or not. It didn't seem to weigh any more than it had when it'd been empty. He gave it a gentle shake, not wishing to alarm or harm anything which might be inside, and was fairly confident that he felt some vague hint of movement from within.

'Best five pounds I ever spent' Tom thought to himself cheerily, before the dawning realisation struck him that he couldn't very well leave the poor little blighter stuck in there all day long on his own. There was simply nothing else for it; he would have to call in to work and let them know that he was going to be even later than usual. Remembering the information that he'd sourced from the day before, he decided to heed the Internet's advice and take a drive to somewhere at least a couple of miles from home to release his catch.

Inside meanwhile, Maurice awoke with a start, sliding unelegantly back and forth, from end to end of the suddenly moving tube.

Tom had given the matter some considerable thought the day before, whilst sitting at his desk, and had already decided on a suitable release point: a large park that he knew of, set among lush green fields and leafy woodland, thinking that this would be a nice place to set the little fellow free. He reasoned that this spot would provide plenty of cover and therefore a greater chance of survival. He was blissfully unaware that he had caught a house mouse, not a field mouse, and that the countryside would be completely alien to it; the equivalent of releasing you or I, alone and unarmed, into the wild African Bush.

Having showered and dressed for work, Tom picked up the telephone and made his apologies to his disconsolate manager before carrying the newly inhabited trap out of the flat to his waiting car, placing it gently on the passenger seat and setting off.

Less than fifteen minutes of ungainly bumping and sliding around inside later, as the vehicle negotiated speedhumps, roundabouts and sped down winding country lanes, the cutting of the engine and slamming of doors signalled Maurice's arrival at his new destination. He was filled with the kind of trepidation barely even imaginable by a package-deal tourist, stepping down from the coach, about to discover their 'allocation on arival'.

Tom placed the trap down on the ground, near a patch of overgrown, tangled weeds and hedgerow, opening the door to grant the tiny captive his freedom once more. But nothing happened. He had expected an immediate, hurried break for glorious freedom but Maurice was hesitant, blinded and disorientated by the sudden burst of daylight and rush of cool, fresh air following such a lengthy period of total, stifling darkness. He remained at the closed end of the chamber for a few minutes, weighing up his options, before being met by the face of his captor, crouching down on the ground to look inside.

Poor little Maurice was caught between a rock and a hard place; or at least, a box and a man's face. He knew, without question, that he couldn't stay in the suffocatingly cramped plastic box forever, not that he really wanted to anyway, but neither did he exactly fondly embrace the prospect of running out into a wild world , far away from home, which he knew absolutely nothing about. Eventually he concluded that, since he would undoubtedly end up leaving one way or another, then it might as well be on his terms, when he was ready and so, bracing himself with a sharp intake of breath, Maurice ran from the trap, scuttling off into the waiting wilderness, straight past the startled human face pressed sideways against the ground; a fugitive, on the run from who knew what.

Route Planner

To begin with, Maurice found himself simply heading hurriedly in the direction that the trap's opening had been facing when he had finally beaten his hasty retreat. Eventually, after only a short while, his pace slowed as he realised that he must surely by now be far enough away to be safely out of human danger, dragging his tiny pink heels to a shuffling crawl and then, at last, a complete stop. He looked all around him in every direction, realising that he had absolutely no idea whatsoever where on earth he was going; the countryside looked the same which ever way he faced and, after turning around in circles several times, trying his hardest to remain calm, he could no longer even be certain of which direction he'd started out in in the first place. He might very well end up walking back exactly the same way that he'd just come. Not that that was necessarily a bad thing you understand. It might even be the right thing to do. He simply didn't know where he was.

His silent melancholy was quickly interrupted by a gaggle of several dozen Canada Geese, whose honking traffic overhead attracted his attention upwards. As he watched them making their way to whatever exotic location it was that they were heading for, or back from, he noticed that they flew in a near perfect V formation, creating the illusion of a single, gigantic, airborn arrow-head, pointing to his left. His heart lifted momentarily. Was it the sign he was looking for? Before he even had a chance to let the idea sink in though, the birds had disappeared, leaving the sky empty once more and poor Maurice wondering if maybe he'd completely imagined the whole thing or, at the very least, its significance. His eyes scanned the air again, seeking another message from above; perhaps a second flock formation which might provide some significant reason to choose one direction in favour of another, some bendy straw at which to feebly grasp, some small ray of hope, however vain. A lone pigeon flapped its way across the otherwise clear, empty, cloudless sky, in exactly the direction from which Maurice had just come; or at least, exactly the direction from which he thought he might have just come and, anyway, in a completely different direction from the way that the geese had been aiming. It really wasn't very much to go on at all, however you dressed it up.

Dejected, his head dropped down, looking at the ground, drumming his toes there as he sought some kind of divine intervention which might provide him with another clue as to the correct route home. The sun was creeping upwards and he watched his own shadow stretch out ever darker and more clearly defined to his left as the power of its rays increased. The exaggerated, charachateurised outline of Maurice's elongated torso, pointy nose and large sloping ears, had created a quite convincing imitation silhouette of an almost road-sign-perfect black arrow. Since he had no reason to go in any other direction and this sign seemed too persuasive to ignore, he opted to acknowledge and accept it, heading off the way that it pointed, keeping his shadow in front of him, perfectly in line with his forward facing body, to ensure that he didn't veer off in any other direction. At least this way he wouldn't just walk around in circles, he guessed, although he hadn't even considered the fact that the sun moved position throughout the course of the day.

Maurice skipped gaily along for a time before a horrible thought suddenly struck him. As the sun rose ever higher in the sky until it was directly overhead, his shadow would shorten until it became non-existent and then his plan would be scuppered. He decided to take a rest and think about what alternative method he might use to determine his chosen path. He tried to think about all the potentially useful information that he'd learned in Geography classes at Mouse School, in the hope that this might yield some new revelation and it wasn't long before one came to him, in a gust of wind. He had an idea which might very well just work. He knew that Tom lived near to the coast and that the air there was cooled by the sea in a form of natural air-conditioning; in fact it was one of the very things that had appealed to the Major about the place when they'd first moved there in the height of an unusually intense but typically brief, week-long British summer heatwave. He knew too that when this water-cooled air met with the drier, warmer air inland, the meeting of different high and low density air pressures often created a fairly strong wind which blew inward from the coast. As his fur and whiskers were ruffled by a sudden stiff puff of breeze, he decided to change course slightly and head directly into the wind, figuring that this ought to mean that he was therefore aiming for the shore. The occasional piece of grit and greenfly in the face and slight drying of his eyes would be a small price to pay for the comfort that he might be heading home. If he could just find his way into a town, he concluded, he could hopefully use his knowledge of the English language to read any road signs that he came across. The beach, by which his family and Tom lived, was a popular holiday resort destination. The Seafront should therefore be well signposted. When he got anywhere near to the shore-line, he would hopefully see and hear seagulls in the air which would help lead him along on the home straight; that was, assuming that he ever made it that far. In the meantime, if he managed to befriend any small birds, tits, sparrows and the like, he might manage to get them to help confirm where it was that he needed to go. He was really on a roll now. The ideas were coming thick and fast. He looked optimistically skyward to see if perhaps there might be some gulls flying overhead already. For all he knew, he might not even be all that far from the beach right now. He didn't see any but he did see one final thing which sealed the deal and helped make up his mind once and for all about which way to head. A long way off, barely visible save for its long downward arcing vapour trail, was the tiny speck of a distant Jumbo Jet. Maurice could see from the angle that it had already begun its steady descent to land. He reasoned that since large planes of this type generally only flew from one country to another, then it would most likely be coming in from warmer climes abroad and hence from over the ocean. If the arrow shape of the plane was pointing down to land then the opposite direction should, logically therefore, be the sea. This merely served to confirm that he should indeed continue on the way that he'd already calculated, except that now he had a long white vapour trail in the sky to follow too, in case the wind should die down, assuming of course that it didn't evaporate too soon, and his hopes along with it.

And so Maurice set about his journey, using that mysterious, instinctive mouse homing-device which had so intrigued Tom; a combination of logic, superstition and good old-fashioned guesswork!

Brody

Maurice rested on a moss covered log by the water's edge, taking in the natural beauty of the ideallic, tranquil scene before him. As the early summer sun came up from behind the trees, the air began to warm, lifting the last of the morning mist to unveil a picture worthy of any Monet masterpiece.

A lone swan waterskied momentarily as it came in to land, large webbed feet skimming along the surface, slowing it gracefully, with the help of majestic outstretched wings, to a regal floating glide; a smooth wake fanning out behind it. Dragonflies divebombed in and out among the reeds, a blur of humming wings and turquoise luminescence; hover flies hung suspended in the air before darting and jerking here and there suddenly like puppets on strings; whirligig beetles spun round and round on the pond's meniscus as if remote control toys operated by a toddler. Waterboatmen skulled past in coxless pairs, as skilfull as any Oxbridge oarsmen and pondskaters danced their sporadic Boleros.   Only the occasional rising bubbles rippling the otherwise unblemished mirror-glass surface hinted at the lives being played out in the aquatic world beneath – a world far more dangerous than Maurice could ever have believed, faced here with such apparent quiet calm and serenity.

"Don't even think about it mate!"

Maurice nearly fell backwards off of the log, the sudden exclamation breaking the silence made him jump so.

"I'm sorry?" he said. "Who's there?"

"Brody" announced the chubby, grizzled little water vole, clambering up the muddy bank and into view on the glistening dew drenched grass at the top. The way he said it suggested that no further explanation really ought to be necessary; as if Maurice should have somehow already heard of him and know exactly what his original outburst was supposed to have meant.

"Oh, erm, I'm Maurice" said Maurice, still somewhat taken aback and not at all sure what his original outburst was suppoosed to have meant. "Don't even think about *what* exactly?"

"Swimming across of course" he replied. "I'm a water vole. Got my Junior Lifeguard Bronze Award and everything. Strongest swimmer you're ever likely to meet, that's for by jiggerdy certain" he boasted "and even I wouldn't chance it."

"Oh, erm, right" said Maurice, a little confused. He wasn't even sure that he had ever been considering swimming across in the first place but he was still curious to know more, especially now that the seed of the idea had been planted.

"Why not exactly?" he asked.

"Lucius" said Brody. Again, he spoke as if this should be all the information that was needed on the subject. Discussion over. Maurice was starting to wonder if he did it on purpose. He suspected that the vole liked the power of having all the answers and making him work for them. Maybe it made him feel more intelligent or important in some way and made up for his tiny size – he was barely any bigger than Maurice, although was considerably more rotund. Maurice still wanted to know more anyway so decided to humour him and play along regardless.

"What's a Lucius?"

"Not *what*." Brodie sighed . "*Who*! He's the monster of the deep. Fifty feet long if he's an inch. Countless victims over the years. Swallows them whole most of the time. See Philippa over there?" he continued, gesturing towards a rather matronly mallard, busy supervising her three fluffy yellow and brown striped ducklings as they stumbled across the sagging water-lilies at the pond's edge. "She had five last week. Strayed too far from the bank during a moonlit midnight swim. Two never made it back." He spoke dramatically, seeming almost to revel in the awful horror of the story and the impact that it might have for a moment, before adding more sombrely "I need to get to the other side myself. See that hole, third from the left?" he pointed to the opposite bank. "That's mine. Panoramic views across the water" he said, trying to impress. Maurice just thought that he sounded like an estate agent. He didn't have the heart, or the petty inclination, to tell him that his own family home, Tom's, had 'Oceanic' Marine glimpses across the Estuary – at least, it did if you were tall (which, clearly, neither of them were), had eyesight like a buzzard (which neither of them did) and stood in exactly the right spot. "Shame I'll never get to enjoy them again" Brody went on, oblivious. "Lucius can detect the smallest vibrations from your feet kicking in the water. His victims don't ever see or hear him coming until it's too late. One minute you're having a nice relaxing dip in the afternoon sun and the next you're gone, fish supper, never to be seen again. There's absolutely no way you'd ever get across to the other side. Not in a dozen years." Which was significantly greater than the longest lifespan of any known mouse or vole ever recorded so may just as well have been a million.

"Why don't you just go around the outside?" asked Maurice, well aware that he might be stating the absurdly obvious.

"Certain death!" Brody explained instantly. He was obviously expecting the question.

"The land to the right and left of us is open grass, see? The weekly lawnmowers keep it closely cropped like a carpet at all times. There's no cover whatsoever and the trees around the perimeter are filled with owls and hawks. You'd be spotted so easily from the air that you might as well cover yourself in mayonnaise and wear a sandwich board reading 'Today's Special'! Not to mention the people and their gormless, yapping dogs romping all about the place.

"Well how did you manage to get over here in the first place then?" enquired Maurice.

"Fell asleep in a pile of leaves, woke up in a wheelbarrow over here. Been working really long hours lately, taking on extra shifts just to make ends meet. Must have been out for the count. Been stuck here ever since." He let Maurice fill in the blanks for himself. "The only alternative is to cross the pond but you'd never get so much as halfway".

"Unless" muttered Maurice, half squeaking to himself and eyeing an unopened can of fizzy drink which had been washed up, presumably dropped into the water by one of the many children who regularly launched their toy boats here during the summer months. He'd been studying it for some time. Long enough, in fact, to make out the words 'Orca-Cola' written along the side – and long enough to notice that it floated.

"Unless?" replied Brody, impatiently "Unless what?" Now it was his turn to have to push for more information.

"Unless" Maurice repeated, pausing unhurriedly in a deliberate attempt to replicate Brody's dramatic style "Unless you didn't have to *swim* across, at all."

"How on earth are you going to get across otherwise? Fly, I suppose!" Brody scoffed, snorting a little.

"You wouldn't have to swim if you had a raft" countered Maurice.

"A raft?" Brody was beginning to make a habit of echoing Maurice and turning everything that he said into a question.

"Yes" elaborated Maurice "If you had a raft, you wouldn't have to put your feet in the water at all."

"And where, pray tell, do you propose to find this imaginary vessel?" quizzed Brody sarcastically, unconvinced.

"Over there" Maurice pointed towards the aluminium can bobbing around at the water's edge. Brody stared at it for a while, gathering his thoughts together before responding.

"How are we supposed to propel it if we don't put our paws in the water? It's not as if it has an outboard motor!" He was quick to point out the glaring flaws in the slowly hatching plan but Maurice could tell from the intrigue in his tone that he was starting to consider the possibility a little more seriously with each new sentence.

"We could use paddles".

"Where on earth are we going to find a set of rodent-sized paddles?"

Maurice was starting to despair of his new accomplice's negativity and lack of innovation.

"We make some. Or we just use something that's already the right sort of size and shape that will do the job just as well."

"Like what?"

"I don't know" sighed Maurice "I've never paddled a cyclindrical, metal raft across a monster filled lake before! Let's just stop wasting time and look for something suitable."

And so, the two new nautical associates set off, searching around the leafy glade beside the pond. It wasn't long before they stumbled across a wooden picnic bench in the middle of a small, sun-lit clearing, beneath which lay a selection of balsa ice-lolly sticks, each half stained orange, red or green by the coloured ices that they'd once supported.

"Perfect!" declared Maurice. They were lightweight, just the right length and flat-sided like a paddle with rounded ends and no sharp corners on which to injure themselves. Maurice even noticed some writing on them. After a bit of analysis he had worked out the words on his paddle, which read:

Q) How do you save a drowning mouse? A) Mouse to mouse resuscitation

Maurice didn't see the funny side.

"We'll take one each, straddle the can for balance and row a side each to keep us going in a straight line" he explained; and off they set with their new makeshift chandlery.

Lucius

Arriving at the shore-line, as they waded in, just beyond the water's edge, straggles of clingy pond-weed tangling at their ankles, causing them to recoil with imagination fuelled terror, the morning calm was broken by the sudden sound of raucous, husky laughter from somewhere just close by. Leaning against a clump of reeds to their right, swaying backwards and forwards significantly more than the reeds themselves, was the glistening figure of a great-crested newt, staring over at them through rolling, blood-shot eyes, pointing rudely in their direction; at least, he was when he could actually maintain his balance long enough without stumbling about all over the place, repeatedly falling backwards, only to be caught and steadied again by another flexing clump of supporting reeds.

"What's so funny?" asked Maurice, turning to Brody for reassurance, more than a little unnerved by the ambiguous, knowing cackle.

"Just ignore him" advised Brody. "That's just Isaac, the local lake lush. Probably only just on his way home from last night".

The newt continued to point and laugh. It wasn't a happy laugh though and was interspersed with the occasional hiccup as he spoke, which, in his present state, seemed almost sufficient on its own to unsteady him enough to fall over.

"Good luck fellas" he slurred "You're gonnna need it ... hic ... if you plan on cross .... hic .... plan on cross .... hic .... plan on crossing on *that* thing. And I should know."

"What does he mean by that?" whispered Maurice, not sure that he really wanted the answer but equally unable to stand the not knowing "Why should he know?"

Brody busied himself with preparing to set sail, preferring to avoid eye contact with Maurice, as if this might somehow cause the details of his following statement to be less real.

"Lost his wife on this pond. Hit him real hard, poor chap. Turned to drink. Developed a chronic fear of water. Not been out of his depth since. Probably drink the whole thing dry if he had his way. Tough break for an amphibian."

"Oh dear" sympathised Maurice "What happened to her?"

If it hadn't been for the task that they were both about to undertake together, Brody would usually have simply delighted in responding to just such a question, striking the fear of God into the little mouse with every minute, macabre detail but, instead, chose to keep his explanation brief, for he knew that the truth of each of his words would only serve to further chill himself too.

"Another light Lucius lunch."

Ignoring Isaacs pleading cries, which had progressed from ignominious taunts to portentous predictions, they resolutely rolled the tin-can into a good spot, aimed it pointing directly towards their target, pushed away until the whole thing was floating and clambered aboard before it drifted away, out of their depth. Neither wanted to spend a second longer than was absolutely necessary with any part of their body suspended in the mud-stirred, murky shallows.

"It doesn't feel very stable" Brody frowned.

"It'll be fine" assured Maurice but, sitting behind Brody, he was frowning too.

During the early stages, they rowed in silence, both too anxious to utter a sound. After every few strokes, Brody would glance round to make sure that his co-pilot was still there and each time would be greeted with a fixed grimace intended, unconvincingly by Maurice, to convey a confident and contented smile. Every time they dipped their paddles into the water, disturbing the smooth surface, they wondered if they would draw them, or their paws, back again.

Sun shone down, warming their already flushed faces, but the air was still relatively cool, with only the very subtlest of breezes blowing at their backs every now and then. The conditions were perfect, endowing them with renewed vigour and, with each succesful stroke of their paddles, their confidence grew, along with their optimism at the prospect of making the potentially fatal trip unharmed. Due partly to this growing excitement and partly as a way of making themselves feel better, they started first humming, then whistling and finally singing and even banging away on the can's surface with their paws like a bongo drum as they took a well earned and much needed rest:

"We are sailing, we are *sailing*, home again, across the sea" It wasn't the sea of course – it was just a pond - but it felt like it to a mouse; or even a vole for that matter.

As the approaching bank loomed ever closer and the trees appeared larger, so too did their exhilarated thumping and singing.

The gift of hindsight would soon reveal that this was not a particularly good idea. Banging an aluminium can, floating in a pool of water, causes vibrations and this, combined with the muted sounds of their singing from above the surface and the stark, contrasting silhouette of their outline against the glistening, sun-kissed backdrop was, unbeknown to them, attracting some serious, unwanted attention from the depths below.

Brody was the first to stop singing, mouth still moving silently for a few seconds longer than the sound, and held up a paw to signal to Maurice that he too should do the same.

"What is it?" whispered Maurice

"Look around us" replied Brody.

"What?" questioned Maurice, "I don't see anything."

"Exactly" said Brody

"I'm not with you." Not for the first time that day, Maurice was confused by the chubby vole's infuriating lack of elaboration. Why did he have to make him beg for every tiny snippet of information? Panic was starting to set in, although he wasn't even yet sure what it was that he was supposed to be worrying about.

"There's nothing to see *anywhere*" Brody explained "I know this place like the back of my paw. Lived here all my life. There's usually always something going on. It's quiet. *Too* quiet. No hustle and bustle. There's not one duck, coot or moorhen on the whole pond. Something's wrong. The only time I've ever seen it like this before was when ..." He stopped in his tracks, gasping at what he saw over his deck-hand's right shoulder. His Adam's Apple rose and fell as he swallowed, a deep, audible gulp, alerting his companion to the possible peril nearby. Maurice could see in Brody's beady little eyes that he'd seen something and, from the look on his face, it wasn't something that he was overly pleased about. His next few words confirmed this.

"We're gonna need a bigger can" he observed, trancelike, still staring fixedly in the same direction.

"Why? What is it?" asked Maurice, trying to keep his voice low and avoid becoming hysterical.

"Dorsal fin"

"How big?"

"Big. Very big."

"Was it....?"

"Yep. It was him alright."

"What do we do now then?" Maurice whimpered.

But they didn't have time to do anything before Lucius circled them again, this time much closer, his huge scaley, serpentine body arcing out of the water, exposing the muscular, mottled killer in all his menacing glory. In reality, he wasn't anything close to the fifty feet length that Brody had spoken of earlier but he was still certainly a monster of record breaking proportions. The wave that he created, caused the can to bob and roll so that it was all that the two unsettled rodents could do to keep from falling into the water and almost certainly the waiting, razor-toothed jaws of the forty-seven pound pike. The can rotated so much that the two sailors had to run on the spot like a circus balancing act, spinning it ever faster and faster until they were quite literally sprinting for their lives, although going nowhere fast. As it moved through the water, the sides became wet all the way around, adding to the already deperate situation as they slipped and stumbled against each other like circus clowns.

Suddenly though, just when all chance of survival had seemed hopeless, their running slowed to a jog, eventually stopping completely as the cylindrical treadmill came to a bobbing halt. As they slumped down exhausted on the metallic surface, gasping and wheezing, Lucius disappeared out of sight.

"That was too close for comfort" wheezed Brody "What are we supposed to do now? We don't have much further to go but we daren't start paddling again or he'll come back for us and next time he'll probably finish the job. I haven't got the energy left to go through all that again. The only reason he went away was because we were lucky

71

enough not to fall in and he eventually lost interest when there were no legs or paddles in the water."

"Well there is now" replied Maurice, more than a little irritated by his companion's unconstructive update.

"Eh? What do you mean?" asked Brody

Maurice pointed at the lolly stick, floating agonisingly slowly away out of reach. In all the commotion, Brody had failed to keep hold of his.

"We couldn't paddle now even if our lives depended on it" Maurice remarked.

"Which they do" Brody reminded him, apologetically.

"We'd just go round and round in circles. I'm sure there's an expression that describes our situation pretty well." Maurice observed. Brody knew what it was too but remained quiet.

The two of them sat there in silence for a while , thoughts and pulses racing, until finally Maurice blurted out "Hold on! I've got an idea."

"Not another hairbrained scheme!" groaned Brody "Your last one nearly got us both killed."

"Yes, but it's also nearly seen you home. Do you have any bright ideas of your own?"

"No" Brody grudgingly admitted.

"Well, you're just going to have to go with mine then, aren't you?"

"I guess I don't really have any choice." He had already resigned himself to the fact.

"Ok, that's settled then. Since there is no plan B, I say we advance straight to plan A." Maurice rubbed his paws together cheerily, revelling in this newfound assertiveness. "You're just going to have to trust me and do exactly as I say." He told Brody to stay down one end of the can whilst he shuffled his way to the other, sat on the edge and dangled his feet over the side, resting them on the ring-pull for support as he proceeded to splash furiously at the water with the remaining lolly stick.

"What the blue blazes are you doing?" squealed Brody, bemused "You'll get us both killed!"

"Just stay where you are and trust me! I know exactly what I'm doing." asserted Maurice.

"You've gone stark raving mad" accused Brody "That's what you've done!".

"Maybe" Maurice had a manic grin on his face, a possessed, devilish look in his eyes "But then again .... maybe not."

Less than half a minute had passed and Maurice was already beginning to tire. The journey across the lake had taken a lot out of him and stirring and slapping the giant lolly stick through the water was hard work, but it would soon pay dividends and achieve the desired results, as Maurice was about to discover. Peering down expectanatly, he saw the huge, dark shadow grow in size, bearing up on him at an alarming rate from below the surface and had just about enough time to swing his legs back up, run to the other end of the can and scream "Jump!" for all his worth as he leapt into the water, dragging his partner in with him.

Lucius hit the can like a torpedo, his powerful jaws clamping down on the soft, aluminium sides like a vice. Flying several feet out of the water and into the air, he crashed back down, tail thrashing wildly, showering the two frantic swimmers as they headed for dry land. All the earlier unsettling of the can had shaken up the soda inside so that it burst through the puncture holes under enormous pressure, exploding fizzy dark-brown liquid into the fish's mouth and down its throat. The can was impaled firmly onto the pike's teeth and no matter how hard he tried, he couldn't shake it free. The more effort he made, the more he merely succeeded in creating an even stronger jet of frothy fluid. Carbonated foam oozed from his gills as he writhed and flipped around in the water until the drink finally lost all of its' fizz; long enough to see the two intrepid mariners pulling their bedraggled bodies, coughing and spluttering, up the muddy bank to the welcoming sanctuary of Brody's riverside apartment.

Magwitch

Maurice waved farewell to Brody and his family, fuelled by the hearty homecoming celebration breakfast laid on for the two of them by his new friend's good lady wife, Ellen. It was already late in the afternoon. They had both slept solidly for nearly twenty four hours, so completely and utterly worn out were they by the previous day's drama.

Today was noticeably cooler than the day before and Maurice wondered if Autumn was now on the turn as he marched along, kicking the first of the approaching season's fallen leaves. He was still light on his feet but had a distinct hint of boldness in his stride that had definitely not been there the day before yesterday. Staying in the tall, unkempt grass close to the edge of the lake, he remembered what Brody had said about the owls and hawks waiting in the trees, although was equally wary of grass snakes which he knew were proficient hunters both in water and on land and favoured this type of terrain. There was simply no getting around it, when you were a mouse, out in the big wide world, nowhere was safe. The list of potential dangers was seemingly endless and Maurice made a mental note to himself not to become too complacent and to remain hidden, out of view as much as possible at all times, as his father had always taught him.

From within the dense copse to his right, Maurice was accompanied as he went by nature's symphony, performed by the local woodland orchestra. Wood pigeons cooed their incessant monologues, providing the wind section from high in the branches and were met with the echo of hammering woodpeckers, taking care of percussion, hard at work nearby. The clack-clacking machine-gun fire of a pair of magpies caused Maurice to glance over in their direction. 'Two for joy' he thought to himself, smiling at but nonetheless emboldened by his own silly superstition. He was happy to take any ray of hope that he could get at the moment. Having lived most of his life in a town, many of the sights and sounds were new to him. He had learned about natural history at school but seeing things in the fur (and feathers) for the first time was quite a new experience altogether and Maurice marvelled at the rich pallet of colours splashed generously all around. Copper-breasted chaffinches hopped from twig to twig as stone-pink jays tinged with pearlescent blue flashes darted in and out of view across his field of vision. Search parties of countless grey squirrels bounded across the ground in every direction, rummaging among the leaf litter for winter supplies while end of season stocks lasted, tails twitching nervously as they kept watch for predators, occassionally scurrying with agile expertise up the side of a tree-trunk at the slightest disturbance. They made Maurice feel better. By his reckoning, two hundred pairs of eyes were surely better than one.

After a while, in the distance, Maurice could make out a large stone building and decided to head in its' general direction. It was the only man-made structure that he'd seen since being dropped off in the middle of nowhere, two days earlier, and he concluded that since he had no other solid leads at the moment, then at least this was a sign that he might be coming to some form of civilization as he knew it. As the sun started to go down, the air quickly cooled and a thick foggy mist descended. Dusk fell and, with it, so too did Maurice's mood. He really didn't relish the idea of having to spend the night outside on his own. He figured that he'd be extremely unlikely to be able to sleep anyway, what with the cold and all the ambiguous night sounds force-feeding his fear, and so decided instead to carry on moving. He'd had so much sleep at Brody's that he wasn't tired anyway.

As the imposing building loomed ever closer, Maurice could make out the burial-parade ground of hundreds of headstones standing to attention all around it and realised, with mixed emotions, that it must be a church. The initial optimism that seeing the structure had brought with it dissipated, like the moon behind a cloud, as the eerie scene ahead gradually unfolded. Dense mist, blown up from the pond by the soughing night wind, swirled around the stone slabs and masonry crosses and pug-nosed greater horseshoe bats squeaked their barely audible, ultra-sonic mutterings and fluttered erratically overhead, changing direction suddenly in pursuit of yet another unfortunate dusty death's head hawkmoth.

Maurice came to a halt, by a clump of deadly nightshade, weighing up the spooky situation, trying to decide what to do for the best. He didn't want the last thing that he ever saw to be a ghostly white figure silently plucking him from the ground and knew from the many horror films that he'd watched lately from behind Tom's breakfast bar, that this was perfect barn owl territory. It wasn't long though before he was woken from deep in his thoughts with a start.

"Psst!" came the stifled hiss from only a few feet away.

Maurice strained his eyes, through the dank air, to make out the glinting edge of metal and a pair of dark eyes reflecting what little moonlight there was right back at him.

"Who's there?" Maurice asked, with more than a slight, uneasy feeling of deja vu.

"Over 'ere boy!" a gruff voice called back.

Maurice was understandably wary and edged nervously forward, trying to get a better look at the unknown quantity.

"Don't worry boy. I can't 'urt ya. I'm trapped."

"Trapped?" confirmed Maurice "What do you mean?"

"Trapped, I tell ya. In a cage. No better'n an animal." He spoke without a hint of irony. "Come closer soze I can get me a better look at ya!"

Maurice crept out of the shadows and as he did so, a break in the evening cloud cast a momentary moonlit eye over the spot in front of him, bathing the cage and its prisoner in monochromatic blue for the briefest blink of a second; long enough to make him jump back again with a start at what he saw.

"You're .... a weasel!" blurted Maurice, eyes wide with fear.

"No boy, I aint no weasel. Does I look like I goes pop? I'm more than twice the size of a weasel!" replied the mysterious figure indignantly.

"Oh. Sorry. A stoat then!" Maurice fired, remembering what he'd learned in class about the differences between the two.

"No boy. Not no ermine-wearing toff neither. I'm twice the size of one o'them tiddlers an'all!"

"An otter?" suggested Maurice, somewhat reticently.

"Are you trying to wind me up boy? A flippin' fish-face of all things!?"

"Pine Marten?" ventured Maurice, more doubtfully than ever, screwing his face up with a wince as he said it, for fear of having made yet another wrong guess. The look on the face he was met with though was enough to give him his answer without any words being necessary (although there were some barely audible under-breath mutterings of 'squirrel-scoffers' and other presumably derogatory mumblings) and so, rapidly running out of ideas, he had one final, tentative stab at "Mon.....goose?" He knew before the word had even finished leaving his lips though that he was clearly way off the mark and wished that he'd just known when to give in and admit defeat.

"Lord 'ave mercy!" cried the unidentified creature in despair "A mongoose! That scourge of a snake in the grass? They don't even live in this 'ere country! Not even the right continent, I'm doubtin'! I'm a mink, aint I, for Pete's sake! Aint it obvious?""

"Oh. Right. Sorry." Maurice apologised again "Now that you've said it, I guess I can see......"

"No 'arm done I s'pose. What's yer name boy?"

"Erm, Maurice sir" answered Maurice impulsively, not at all sure that maybe he oughtn't to have offered some sort of pseudonym instead "What's yours?"

"Magwitch, ever at your service boy" replied the mink, stretching his paw out through the bars for Maurice to shake.

"Erm, I don't mean any disrespect sir" stumbled Maurice, staring at the outstretched claws, "but don't mink usually, erm, eat mice?"

"That they do my boy, that they do" confessed Magwitch "but not this 'ere involuntarily veganised vagabond you see before ya. I'm stuck in this 'ere cage, no 'arm to anyone, not man nor beast. You wouldn't begrudge a poor, solitarily confinated soul an ounce of friendliness and compassion in 'is hour of most desperate need, now would ya?"

Maurice knew only too well the anguish that came of being imprisoned, awaiting an uncertain fate. He offered his own tiny, inferior pink paw in return.

Magwitch grabbed it firmly and yanked Maurice towards the bars of the cage so that their noses were almost touching and he could smell the mink's metallic, bloody breath.

" Now then my boy" Magwitch snarled " I needs ya to run a small errand and 'elp me escape this 'ere contraption see?"

"How am I supposed to do that?" murmured Maurice

"Don't you worry yer little 'ead about the whys and the wherefores. I'll tell ya what to do and you just do it see?"

"But, pardon me for asking sir; just supposing I do manage to help get you free" posed Maurice "How do I know that you won't eat me afterwards?"

"You don't, do ya boy!" he cackled "But ya don't really 'ave a choice, see? I 'ave 'ere in my company an acquaintance hidden away out of view but watching you this very minute. Now, he's an awful fella. Vicious. Not nearly so polite an' agreeable as me he aint. Has a way of finding you in the dead of night if he so makes it 'is business to do so. A mouse may be warm in bed, pull the covers over his 'ead but into your room he'll softly creep and eat yer 'eart and liver out! Now, you promise to get what I ask for and come back and I'll make sure you stays safe an' he leaves you alone in return. Deal?" and he spat a globule of pink spittle into his palm and held it back out through the bars for Maurice to do the same; he didn't make it sound like a question with any room for negotiation on the answer. 'No deal' was clearly not an option for this accidental contestant.

Maurice wondered why, if he had such a tough, terrible friend nearby, Magwitch didn't just ask *him* to help free him instead and so put this to him.

"Far too big" explained Magwitch "He'd never make it into the chapel and get what I need, without being seen. You're tiny. You could do it easy."

Maurice still wasn't convinced that there really was an accomplice hiding in the sidelines anywhere at all but did he really want to take that chance and spend the rest of his life looking over his shoulder, worried for the safety of his internal organs? He wasn't certain enough that he was prepared to gamble his life on it.

"Ok then" he agreed, already beginning to wonder if he might live to regret his decision "Deal."

"Say 'heaven strike me dead if I don't'" insisted Magwitch as an additional clause to the arrangement. Maurice repeated the pledge but wasn't overjoyed at the phrase.

Mission Impossible

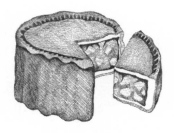

Magwitch had asked Maurice to break into the priest's quarters and find him some food and something with which to help lever open the trap door. Maurice wasn't convinced that either of them would be strong enough to crowbar open a steel-sprung trap-door, even with the help of an imaginary extra friend, but he wouldn't have the poor soul starve to death so embarked on the mission regardless.

Tiptoeing across the cemetery, he used the deep shadow of the many memorials as cover, leaning up against each one, pausing to catch his breath before making a dash for the next. At one stop, he remained there long enough to make out the engraving which, beneath the deceased's name and dates, read: 'Son to a loving mother, father and two brothers.' Maurice wondered wistfully if he would ever make it home again. He wondered how long he would be gone before his family gave up all hope of ever seeing him again. That was assuming that they had hoped for his return in the first place. But most of all, he wondered if his father would want the same thing written on *his* headstone if he, Maurice, were to be presumed dead and given a corpseless funeral. The haunting screech of an owl, from beyond the trees, soon spurred him on though with an even greater sense of urgency until he very soon found himself, back pressed, panting, against the cobbled wall of the church. A few metres to his right, he saw the faintest shafts of light, accentuated by the foggy evening, indicating the edges of the thick, iron-hinged oak door to the vicarage. Edging his way along, staying as close to the safety of the wall as possible, he was soon standing on the rough coir welcome mat on the oversized stone door-step; the word 'welcome' set invintingly into it, Maurice took the time to decipher. Encouraged by this and the warm air currents emanating from the fire-lit room within, he used every ounce of his available strength, sinewy tendons bulging in his neck, dragging the mat back away from the ancient door to reveal a gap at its base, just large enough for him to squeeze underneath.

On entering the open plan living quarters, he took in the layout of the room; a large lounge with an impressive

Inglenook stone fireplace dominating one whole wall, a charred log spitting and crackling on a pile of glowing ash and embers; the furniture, a mismatch of worn but comfortable looking chairs, covered with patchwork blankets and assorted throws to hide their age; an elderly, ruddy faced gentleman with a bald liver-spotted head and overgrown, whispy white sideburns, dressed all in black, snored in the corner, an abandoned biro lieing beneath his dangling fingers on the floor beside him, waiting to be retrieved to finish the second half of the crossword on the back page of the crumpled newspaper draped across his lap; an old-fashioned radio, a wireless, played classical music and Maurice was glad of the noise to cover the sound of his movements.

Happy that the coast was clear, he made his way across the ornate woven rug and onto the cold stone floor, into the hallway. Peering into each room that he came to, he found first a bedroom, then a bathroom. As he came to the final room at the rear of the small property, rounding the door frame and entering, his impending glee at successfully making it all the way to the kitchen, and hopefully the food, was replaced immediately with a sinking feeling at what he saw. Standing on the floor in front of him were two bowls, one filled with a meat filled jelly and small fish-scented biscuits, the other with water. The word 'Charlie' had been written in a child-like scrawl on the side of one in thick black marker pen. Neither looked as though it had been touched, which hopefully meant that their intended recipient was not at home at the moment.

Yet. He cast a nervous sideways glance at the cat-flap in the door right by his side.

Maurice realised that he would have to work fast. It was bad enough being called 'Cat Food' all the time at school; he didn't much relish the prospect of earning the title for real. He quickly spotted the walk-in larder and, after sorting through the many jars, tins and bottles, managed to locate a large pork pie wrapped in thin grease-proof paper which he was easily able to gnaw at and tear through to get at the stodgy contents inside. He guessed that Magwitch would probably not appreciate anything vegetarian so made sure to choose something nice and meaty for him to eat. Better that than himself, he thought as he broke off a sizeable chunk, as large as he could carry, and set off about the cottage to look for a possible substitute crowbar. Not that he had any idea how he was going to manage to carry such an item even if he did find it. After at least half an hour, which felt more like a lifetime, of frantic searching, he found his way back into the bathroom. The cupboard door beneath the sink had been left ajar, revealing a shelf overflowing with all manner of assorted pharmaceutical paraphernalia. Maurice found a jar of Vaseline and thought about greasing the bars of the cage so that Magwitch could squeeze through them but then remembered that the cage was constructed of a fine-knit mesh; not thick bars. Even he himself wouldn't be able to squeeze through a space that small. 'That's another fine mesh you've got me into' he thought, unsure where he'd heard it before, but chuckling to himself anyway. 'Hold on a second. A *fine* mesh. Not thick bars. Instead of trying to use brute strength to lever open the trap-door, why didn't they cut through the wall of the cage instead?' Excited once again by his own genius, he began tossing aside flannels, cotton buds, combs and ointments in his quest for a suitable tool. His hopes were raised temporarily by the discovery of a pair of stainless steel toe-nail clippers but he wasn't sure that Magwitch would have the strength to squeeze them together hard enough to break through metal and so continued looking. And then he saw it. It might just work. It wouldn't need a huge amount of brute strength either; just some time and a bit of patience. The metal nail-file was small and light enough for him to carry too. He grabbed it up under his spare arm, the chunk of pork pie wedged under the other, and stepped out from inside the cupboard.

The fat ginger tom stood in the doorway, a salivating grin fixed firmly on its face. Maurice had become so frenzied in his search for a cutting tool that he'd been oblivious to the considerable racket that he was making. Why didn't he ever know when to stay quiet? His excited noise making was going to be the death of him yet. The Major had always ranted on about not being seen; why had he never mentioned anything similar about not being heard? The resident church cat had been waiting patiently for him to come out. On finally seeing him, it didn't waste a second, pouncing through the air at little Maurice, needle-like claws splayed out for the kill. Maurice dove to one side, so narrowly avoiding the attack that he felt himself brushed by the ferocious feline's whiskers. As it slid past on the surface of the bathroom's laminate flooring, swiping out wildly again like some feral Freddie Kruger, Maurice instinctively held the nail file out in a vain effort to shield himself from the onslaught, accidentally stabbing it deep into the padded base of the pussy's paw in the process. Ignoring the agonising high-pitched miaows, he seized his chance, ran for the door, skidding into the hallway and bolted for the lounge. The cat had already spun around and was now chasing, hot on his heels, a severe limp now allowing Maurice just the advantage that he needed to make it to the gap under the front door and slide safely out of harm's way. As he ran again for the shadow of the nearest tombstone, Maurice heard the muffled thud of the moggy as it skidded heavily into the solid door and, grinning wryly, wondered how many lives mice had. He'd certainly used up at least three already.

Having successfully run the graveyard gauntlet for a second time, Maurice finally made it back to the cage, baring his ill-gotten gains. On seeing him appear over the brow of the slope, Magwitch could barely contain his excitement and paced backwards and forwards like a caged lion, unable to stand still for a second.

"I couldn't find a jimmy but I found this instead" Maurice held up the nail-file, passing it through the wire mesh.

"Even better, even better!" was Magwitch's rasping verdict as he snatched it roughly from his paws. "And what of the food boy?"

"I got you this" offered Maurice, pushing the crusty baked pie up against the bars.

"You done well my boy. Very well indeed. Make a thief of you yet boy!" Magwitch congratulated him with guttural laughter, greedily breaking pieces off and shoving them ravenously into his mouth, crumbs spraying everywhere as he spoke.

"Please sir" interrupted Maurice, pleased with the reaction that his efforts had achieved and thinking that now might be a good time to bring it up "Will there be anything else sir? If you have no further use for me, then I'd very much like to be on my way. My parents will be worried sick about me." He hoped that saying it out loud might make it so.

"Of course, of course" dismissed Magwitch, not really paying atttention and already busy at work with the file. Maurice reckoned that he would probably have agreed to anything at that particular moment, so absorbed was he in the task at hand. Maurice didn't need to be told twice.

"Well, erm, goodbye then" he said, uncertainly.

"Bye boy" Magwitch didn't even look up. Maurice doubted very much if it was the first time that he'd ever escaped from imprisonment in a locked cell.

Jethro

As day broke, Maurice breathed a sigh of relief, realising that he had made it safely through another night in one piece. As the dawn chorus sprang into life, the seasonal calls of cuckoos, collared doves and the awakening chirrups of crickets rubbing their hind legs together provided the soundtrack for this chapter, setting the mood for the morning and bringing with it the good weather. For as far as his eyes could see, Maurice was wrapped in a multi-coloured, terra-cotta, mustard, khaki and taupe, autumnal patchwork of agricultural British countryside, reaped and sewn, strimmed flat or overgrown, set among expansive undulating hills which, among this and their many other outdoor pursuits, also meandered, rolled and roamed. Giant cotton reels of bailed hay littered the golden patches. In the distance, a tractor ploughed its way through a neatly rutted, chocolate mahogany field, mocked as it went by a murder of ravenous crows, taking advantage of the leather-faced farmer's toil in the soil to cash in on the banquet of fat, juicy worms being exposed invitingly in the overturned earth behind him. Then, as if attempting to prove some puerile point, they would flap away, invariably coming to rest on the outstretched, sack-cloth sleeves of a nearby scarecrow, where they greedily devoured their slimy, squirming booty in full, defiant view of the driver; their winter-reminiscent 'craw craw' further noisily adding vilifying insult to visual injury.

Maurice continued to trudge onward, eventually stopping at a small fresh-water stream which might have been man-made but appeared to provide a convenient natural border between fields of different kinds of cereal. Male sticklebacks darted against the current, oxygenating their gills, inflamed red bellies placing their piscine lonely hearts ads, hopeful of attracting any passing female who might also be fin-loose and fancy-free and broody for roe of her own. Sitting at the brook's edge, Maurice leaned over, looking down at his rippled reflection in the gently running water. Although he looked extremely tired, Maurice felt more alive right now than he had done in a long time. Jumping down from the low bank, he washed his face and quenched his thirst, though not necessarily in that order, before setting off through a field of mature wheat, figuring that this would be the safest place to stay hidden as he travelled.

After a couple of hours of negotiating his way through various neighbouring chequerboard fields of wheat, corn and maize, the little mouse was absolutely exhausted. He'd discovered that the concealment which the cereal offered him, came at a hefty price. Because he couldn't simply walk in a straight line as he would out in the open, due to having to weave his way through the tall stalks, he was covering twice the distance that he would have if he'd gone direct, as the crows did. He wasn't used to physical exercise and wished that he'd listened to his father more in the past; he'd certainly be a lot fitter and managing much more easily now if he had. He sat down in a shaded area, where he felt that the plantation was particularly dense, and leant back against a stem to take a rest. Within minutes he was slumped, head and shoulders hanging forward, chest rising and falling deeply, fast asleep, oblivious to the world around him.

Eyelids flickering, body twitching, his dreams were of Magwitch's evil unseen accomplice, sneaking into his room at home whilst he lay in bed trying to get to sleep. As he attempted to hide away under the bedding, a shadow crept up the length of his body, over his head and onto the wall behind him, revealing the outline of a huge mouse-eating mink-monster. 'Oh no, you're not going to sleep' came the demonic voice as Maurice quivered and quaked where he lay. A huge, clawed hand on his shoulder made him recoil with fear, attempting to escape the evil clutches of the hateful heart and liver burglar and, as he did so, he woke himself with a start, escaping from his own dream in the process. Only inches from his face, was another, as small as, if not smaller than, his own, a tiny wheatsheaf hanging out of one corner of his mouth, looking at Maurice, a tiny mouse-claw on his shoulder shaking him awake.

"Oh no. You're not going to sleep. Not now. Not here, my lovely" the voice was saying. "Why you must be mad as a March hare, you must – though, don't tell him I said, mind!" he glanced furtively around, as if to suggest that the subject of his conversation may be within elongated earshot at this very moment, before continuing, the back of his right paw rested against the left side of his face for added secrecy "He'd box my ears for me, so he would. Box both our ears for that matter if he so much as even suspected we was talking about him" "Either mad, stupid or brave, you must be. Or both!"

Even half asleep still, Maurice wondered how he could use the word 'both' when referring to three options but felt that it would be impolite and perhaps counter productive to mention this grammatical indiscretion so soon in their relationship.

"You'd never last 'til lunchtime. Well, maybe you would, maybe you would – but *you'd* be lunch" he lectured on in his thick, West-Country accent. "There's snakes and hawks and weasels and all sorts roaming these here fields. You can't be leaving yourself all wide open on the ground like that; crazy grockle!" This was all sounding worryingly familiar. He'd heard all these warnings before from Brody. It was tough being a mouse.

"I'm just really terribly tired" croaked Maurice, almost too worn out to speak. "I've been up all night I'm afraid and I just needed to close my eyes for a few minutes; but I must have been more tired than I thought because it seems I fell asleep almost immediately." He went on to explain the events of the previous night as further justification for his fatigue-induced, field-survival faux pas.

"Fair enough. Well, I guess we should get you some rest then, shouldn't we? Come with me lad! You can stay at ol' Jethro's place until you feel up to moving on" he offered, referring to himself in the third person which, again, Maurice found to be a quite unusual way of going about conversing with a newcomer but thought better of bringing it up at this time, so early on in their encounter; and, with that, Jethro proceeded to climb expertly straight up the very stem which Maurice had collapsed against only a little while earlier to take a break. The vibration must have informed the little harvest mouse of the visitor at the foot of the vertical path to his front door.

Maurice tried to follow but didn't have the strength in his upper body to pull himself up. He managed to get a few inches off of the ground but then just clung on for dear life, physically drained, not wishing to drop back down and waste the effort that he'd already put in to get this far, but not having the energy, or physicality, to go any further. Climbing the shoe-lace in PE classes at school had never been his strong point. Maybe if he'd attended Mouse Cadets in the past, like his father had hoped, he'd be having less trouble now.

"Just wrap your tail around the stalk next to you for extra grip!" called down the harvest mouse, from the entrance to a perfectly round, tennis-ball sized nest, about half-way up the stem. Maurice didn't really understand what he meant by this. How was he supposed to wrap his tail around anything when he couldn't let go of the stalk to wrap it anywhere without falling back down. He needed both front paws to hang on with, and was even using the insides of his feet for a little extra support. He pointed this out to his instructor.

"No, not with your paws" came the new guidance "Just use your tail to grip with and take some of the effort away from the rest of your limbs!"

"I don't understand what you're saying!" called Maurice, becoming frustrated and irritable from tiredness. "Can you please come down and show me?"

The harvest mouse climbed effortlessly out of his raised country cottage and down the stem like a fireman down a pole. "Like this" he demonstrated, climbing back up again with consummate ease; and that's when Maurice understood why he couldn't do the same. The harvest mouse's tail actually gripped the vegetation with a life all of its own, just like a fifth limb.

"How does it do that?" asked Maurice, unable to hide the fact that he was, though it pained him to admit it, impressed.

"Oh, my tail do you mean?" he asked, feigning an air of casual surprise "Does yours not do it then?" he looked down at Maurice's hanging, lifeless little thread of a specimen. "No, of course it doesn't. How silly of me! I just takes it for granted sometimes, I does. The field mice are extremely envious and resentful too occassionally" (Maurice was neither), "but the way I see it, it's nature's compensation for my being so small. What's yours?" he asked tactlessly, and Maurice wasn't entirely sure if it was meant as a deliberate put down because he'd finally met someone almost his own size that he could pick on. A classic case of LMS (Little Mouse Syndrome), he suspected.

"Well, I suppose I am quite intelligent" said Maurice, modestly.

"Well so am I, so am I" dismissed the harvest mouse " But I bet you wish you had a grippy tail too, like me, don't you?"

"Prehensile" answered Maurice

"Eh? Pre-what?" queried his companion.

"Pre-hen-sile" Maurice reiterated, deliberately emphasising the syllables idiotically slowly for Jethro's benefit. It means 'capable of grasping. Or perhaps you'd prefer 'grippy'?'"

"Yes, well, whatever" Jethro was dismissive once more, disgruntled at the minor intellectual defeat, but unlikely to be patronised so easily without a fight. "Well how's about I let you hang on to my 'pre-hen-sile'" he emphasised it back even more slowly just for good measure "tail, instead, if I lower it down and then I'll pull you up. I take it that your claws, at least, are 'capable of grasping'?" he mocked still further, turning Maurice's own condescension against him and scoring back yet more petty points in the process.

"Yes. They are" replied Maurice wearily, conceding defeat, too tired to care about winning the harvest mouse's silly word game battle. "Thank you"

Within a few minutes, the totally worn out little house-mouse was curled up, all warm and cosy, inside the neatly woven little hand-thatched harvest-house, watched over with caring concern, despite his brash ways in conversation, by the little golden-coated good Samaritan.

"I'm Maurice, by the way" muttered Maurice, just about managing to get the whole sentence out as he drifted off to sleep, saved from physical collapse for the second time in as many days by a fellow rodent's kind hospitality.

The next day and Maurice had awoken, surprised to find Jethro gone, already out at work in the fields somewhere, nearby a hearty breakfast of dry cereal (you try milking a cow when you're as small as a harvest mouse!), mainly seeds and grain, gathered and laid on for him by his absent little harvest host who had seemed so antagonistic and argumentative at first meeting. Maurice made a mental note never again to judge a book by its cover. His saviour must have been up extremely early to collect all of this lot, Maurice observed, a little shocked and frankly mildly embarrassed at the inaccuracy of his first impression but then immediately just as annoyed with himself for being so surprised, when he remembered also that Jethro had not only given him a roof over his head for the night and single-handedly pulled him up by his tail like a dead-weight, he had probably also saved his life by not leaving him to sleep, exposed, on the ground where he first found him. If it wasn't for his agricultural alter-ego, he might not be here now to see the sun shining in the sky, albeit already heading for the horizon once more. He had slept well into the afternoon.

The way down from the temporary, spherical country retreat required significantly less effort than the way up had and Maurice descended to the ground in exactly the same expert fire-mouse way that Jethro had; or at least that's what he'd have had anyone believe if they'd asked. His departure was really rather clumsy if the truth be known. Climbing out of the nest had taken a number of attempts before deciding on which way round he should be facing and which leg should go first and so on and so forth. When he did finally manage to get out and onto the main exit stalk, he'd held on so tightly for fear of falling what looked, from his vantage point, like more than the three feet that it actually was, that he'd sort of juddered down rather than sliding in a single, silky, fluid movement such as Jethro had. So much so in fact, that he'd actually suffered a few minor friction burns by the time that he reached the ground, but fortunately there was no real significant harm done.

With a belly full of energy-giving sustenance and a heart full of joy at surviving another night out, away from home, Maurice began the long trek through the fields ahead of him.

His joy, however, was to be short lived. The sun was setting again already.

(Now I'll be honest and confess that, in the interests of creative enhancement, I did, at one point, upon arriving here at this closing juncture and recognising the relative lack of any intricacy of plot to the chapter, consider showing a little poetic licence and regaling the reader with the nail-biting tale of a dramatic close escape from an approaching combine harvester, with our epony-mouse hero rescuing Jethro at the last possible moment from the impending, corn-spitting, gnashing, mechanical jaws of death, in return for the generous, altruistic hospitality that he had shown his unexpected arrival; but, not wishing to tempt fate, since nothing of the sort actually happened and this chapter went by relatively smoothly and without hiccup, I believe I shall leave it there.)

Erin

Weaving his way through the last few centimetres of corn, theatrically parting the final ears like a curtain, Maurice stepped out onto the concrete stage and into the orange spot-light of the street lamp-post, illuminating downwards in an inverted pyramid of speckled drizzle. Having slalomed his way across a huge area of tall, unbroken crop-land, unaided by a starless sky overhead, he had completely lost his bearings and couldn't be at all certain whether he'd managed to keep walking in the direction that he'd originally set off in. He looked first to his left and then to his right for inspiration, but was met only with an unbroken, heavily tree-lined pavement, bordering the fast B road, stretching out in either direction for as far as the eye could see. Looking at the field bordering the pavement opposite, he decided that he was probably better off climbing down from the curb at his feet and crossing the road, in order to continue on in what he hoped was still a straight line. He stared down at the ground and noticed, with some surprise, that the artificial light at his back was creating a tall, thin shadow, stretching out in front of him, forming the almost exact shape of a pointing hand, with his ears and pointed nose as the index finger. It was another sign, just as the sun had made when he'd first been setting out on his epic journey. Again, in normal circumstances, Maurice was not by nature a superstitious mouse but, given his current predicament, he was more than happy to grasp any positive omen that came along with both paws.

Having just about firmly made up his mind to cross the tarmac divide, he noticed an irregularity in the otherwise evenly spaced white lines running down the centre of its surface. As his eyes adjusted to the new light conditions, a morbid explanation came to him. Roadkill. In fact, closer inspection and a short walk up and down in either direction, along the footpath, revealed numerous dark breaks in the white lane divides. Maurice was horrified to discover that the carriageway was absolutely littered with the flattened, disfigured outlines of all manner of once living rural fauna. There was an ex-bird; a once garrulous, colourful crow, now silenced, recognizable only by the most delicate of downy pink and blue feathers, left still standing here and there, rising out of the gravel and stirring in the gentle breeze; environmental motorway objecters in defiant, peaceful protest. These were interspersed with a selection of now two-dimensional mammals, clearly all once endowed with the exact same gritty determination as Maurice now had, to traverse this deadly Route 666. He wondered just how dangerous it could really still be. Most of these victims looked as though they'd been taken some time ago, perhaps when more traffic used this journey, before the newer, larger and faster motorways had been built, destroying everything in their path and dissecting the countryside into clinical geometric shapes. He guessed, too, that it must be quite late by now and knew from having listened in the past to the sounds of distant traffic, from the comfort of his bed at home, that the roads became less busy as the hours of early morning approached. Maybe he was worrying unnecessarily, just as his father often did.

The sudden glare of a motorist, roaring into view over the brow of the hill, headlights set to full-beam, dazzled Maurice; so much so that he was temporarily blinded, helpless for a moment. The vehicle raced past with such ferocity that he was knocked almost off of his feet by the rush of wind created, buffeting him backwards until his imminent fall was steadied by the vegetation behind. Maurice patted himself down to shake the exhaust, road and tyre dust from his sooty face and chest, rubbing his blackened eyes with fisted paws before walking back to the edge of the curb. He peered over the lip, looking down at the short drop, small enough even for him to jump easily down, and accepted his own verdict that he might just as well have been standing at the edge of a cliff looking down into an abyss, so foolhardy would it have been to proceed any further. No sooner had this thought popped into his head than it was reinforced by a brawny, chunky-tyred motorbike racing over the hill with such kamikaze aggression that it pulled an unintentional wheelie, nearly taking off into the air completely. Howling past him at an incredible rate of knots, it spun little Maurice around, a full three hundred and sixty degrees, right there on the spot where he stood; disorientating him so much for a moment that he didn't even get a look at the motorcycle's rear registration plate, 'TH15 W4Y', disappearing off into the darkness. He stepped back a few paces from the six inch high precipice, smoothing his disshevelled fur and whiskers with a few sweeps of his fore-paws over the backs of his ears to the end of his pink felt-pen-nib nose.

He thought, ironically, how similar was his current predicament, compared with the earlier challenge of crossing the pike pond and wished that he had some company here with him right now with which to share this dilemma, as he'd had then. He thought affectionately of antagonistic little Brody and what a gargantuan Goliath the two of them had successfully slain together; a truly monumental achievement. He envied him being indoors right now with all the tender love and warmth of his family and thought of how at home Brody's wife had made him feel. He remembered how amazing it had felt to play the part of the triumphant returning warrior for the first time in his life, as he and Brody had bragged of their heroic exploits. Exaggerating and selectively omitting in places, they'd conveniently failed to mention certain small details, such as their splapstick-slipping, clown-like clumsiness on the can or the abject terror that they'd both felt throughout the entire episode. Maurice didn't care though. These were merely trivialities. Details. It had felt good. Really good. At home, he'd always been a sore disappointment to his father where bravery was concerned. He thought of the impressive spread laid on for him when he'd awoken, having been left to lie-in for as long as he needed. His tiny tummy lurched and gurgled at the thought of food. All the vigorous exercise and belly-bursting adrenalin of the day had worked up quite an appetite and he was famished again already. He wished that he'd at least kept a chunk of pastry for himself from the savoury pie that he'd stolen for Magwitch and wondered if, mathematically, that would have cancelled out the guilt of his theft. If he'd stolen a piece of a pie which he'd already stolen earlier from somebody else, then that was two negatives - and that made a plus, didn't it? Taking his share would have been easy. Magwitch would have taken ages to saw through the metal wires and most of the pie had been on the outside of the cage. Oh well. Too late now. He'd had other things on his mind at the time; like not getting eaten himself for a start. And there was always the possibility of Magwitch's still as yet unconfirmed partner in crime coming after him for having breached the terms of their verbal contract. That alone had been enough of a deterrent at the time and, even now, away from the scene, the thought knotted his stomach, caused his mouth to become dry and so at least served to quell his appetite a little. No, with hindsight, he had probably done the right thing after all.

Comforted by the acknowledgement of the good common sense that had so far prevailed, Maurice stopped day-dreaming and aimed to walk along the toe-path until he might find a bridge or any other alternative way of getting himself across the road. He chose left, since that was the direction in which the two speeding vehicles had been heading and because he had no other more profoundly significant reason on which to base his decision.

Staying close to the grassy border, intermittently fading from amber to grey as he repeatedly passed from street-light to shadow, to street-light, to shadow, he would pause every so on, comical, disproportionately large, velvety ears flicking in every direction like satellite-dish spy scanners, trying to identify the many ambiguous rustling sounds coming at him from out of the depths of the night. Rounding the first bend that he came to, he was encouraged by a familiar sight a little way ahead. On either side of the road were two facing rows of predominantly glass-fronted buildings, which would have been displaying their wares had it not been so dark inside. The only light came from the street-lights reflecting on their polished surfaces and this just made it even harder to see what was being sold within without cupping paws against the glass and peering through them. Not that there was any realistic chance of Maurice ever finding out anyway. He wouldn't even have been able to reach the lower-level window sills. The approach to the small parade of shops consisted of an area of slightly lumpy open village green and immaculately tended flower-beds flanking each pavement. About halfway along this stretch, stood a pair of tall aluminium gateposts, each decorated atop with a metal surround encasing an emerald light, which Maurice presumed were intended to represent some kind of ornamental entranceway to the tiny, remote village high street. As he neared these faux village gate-posts, he became increasingly convinced that he could see something moving up ahead, just at the base of one of them. At first he thought that he must surely be imagining things - it had been a long day after all – and if it hadn't been for the irregularity with which it moved, Maurice could have sworn that he was watching a slightly misshapen ball being bounced, as if by an invisible basketball player, although it was actually probably closer, in dimension, to the size of a baseball. The grunting, snuffling object, about four times the size of Maurice himself, something akin to a large pine cone, leapt persistently straight up into the air, landing on the same spot just long enough each time to propel itself straight back up again, as if on a coiled spring. The prickly figure seemd oblivious to Maurice, standing there, quite close by now, silently watching in transfixed fascination.

"Evening" he announced, finally.

The hedgehog's manic pogo came to an abrupt halt as she curled up tightly into a ball, mid-leap, landing with an ungainly bounce and rolling off the edge of the curb, into the gutter, saved from a potentially fatal pancake fate by the sloping camber of the road.

"Sorry" Maurice was not particularly pleased with his introduction.

"Are you trying to give me a heart attack?" panted the un-coiling animal, struggling to get her words out between gasps of breath, whilst pulling herself back up onto the pavement, hind-legs kicking at the air briefly as she scrabbled undaintily to get a foothold. Maurice thought that she looked like she might have been close to having one anyway, rom the solitary aerobic workout that she'd just been having, but thought it might be impolite to say so at such an early juncture in their relationship. "No, I was just ..." he offered weakly, before being interrupted.

"Well, you're going the right way about it if you are" she went on "Creeping up on young ladies in the middle of the night. You should be ashamed of yourself."

"I did say I was sorry" said Maurice humbly. He supposed that she was right to be annoyed, although was not so sure that she was necessarily as young as she apparently believed herself to be.

"I should think so too" she continued to berate him. "A right sorry state of affairs it is when you can't be left alone to go about your private business without being harrassed by love crazed perverts" she lectured. "Whatever is this world coming to?"

Maurice looked at her intently and thought that she was perhaps overestimating the impact of her appeal to the opposite sex. He'd already gotten off on the wrong foot though so decided not to say so. "I'm Maurice" he informed her, with as much forced charm as he could muster. "What's your name?"

"My goodness, you just don't know when to give up do you? I'm Erin, if you will insist on knowing, but it really makes no difference. I'm afraid I'm simply not interested, thank you very much. I'm flattered and all that, truly I am" she effected a weary tone, as if she had to go through this tiresome process of administering rejection on an all too regular basis "but you're not my type. Now why don't you do us both a favour, cut your losses and run along like a good little mouse."

Maurice was indignant at this unwarranted rudeness. "Now look here" he answered "I'm sorry if I scared you. Truly I am. I can assure you that my intentions were entirely honourable. There's no need to be so hostile. You're really not my type either. Goodnight."

Maurice turned majestically, as if to continue on his way, before feeling Erin's stumpy claws on his shoulder, spinning him around.

"What do you mean, I'm not your type? Why on earth not? What's wrong with me?" enquired the hedgehog, indignantly. "Got tickets on yourself, I suppose? Bit of a ladies' mouse? Well, you're nothing special Casanova, believe me."

"Nothing. You're .....very... attractive" Maurice exaggerated "It's just that....."

"I knew it! You *were* coming onto me after all, you filthy little fur ball!"

"Look!" blurted an exasperated Maurice "You are *so* not my type. You couldn't be further from the truth. I wouldn't be interested in you in *that* way if you were the last hedgehog on earth. I was just curious to know what you were doing, that was all!"

"Oh" Erin replied "Well, why didn't you just say so, mister stroppy whiskers? Somebody obviously got out of bed the wrong side this morning. Men!"

Maurice made as if about to try and explain that he had meant to do precisely that all along, before being shouted at and slandered so, but decided that it would have been highly unlikely to get him anywhere, so instead just let out a surrendering sigh. "Well?" he pressed.

"I was trying to reach the initiator" explained Erin.

"The inishy ..... what?"

"Yes. Just there." she pointed upwards to the small white button set into the base of a black box made of what looked like glass or plastic, or both, mounted about three feet up the thick metal pole "So that I can get safely across the road, unharmed"

"Oh." Given this new snippet of ambiguous information, Maurice was suddenly even more interested than he had been before. "And what does it do exactly?"

"It activates the protective forcefield. Cars, bikes, even lorries can't penetrate it." From the smug way that she spoke, anyone would have thought that she'd made it herself. Maurice was dubious.

"Protective forcefield?" It was quite clear from his tone that he didn't altogether believe her. "How does it work then?"

"I don't know!" snapped Erin, as prickly as ever "I'm not a scientist. I just know that it works, that's all."

"And how *exactly* do you know this?" Maurice asked.

"I've seen it with my own two eyes; and I'm nocturnal." Maurice failed to see the relevance of this second detail. He wasn't sure that it necessarily meant that she had good eye-sight; or even that she didn't tell lies for that matter.

It just meant that she could see in the dark — that was, assuming that her eyesight was ok in the first place."

"Well, what have you seen then?" he was keen to get to the bottom of the matter either way.

"I've seen people use it. Lots of times. They just press the initiator" (Maurice felt quite certain that she had probably applied this word to the simple plastic button herself to make it, and herself, seem more interesting), "then there's a short pause, followed by some high-pitched beeping and, after a few seconds of powering up, the emerald lights change to amber and then ruby to indicate that the invisible force-field is fully activated. Simple as that."

Maurice had to admit that her account was pretty convincing and she seemed genuinely to believe what she was saying but he still had some further questions which needed answering. "You said that you'd seen it with your own eyes. How do you know that it's operating if it's invisible?"

"I didn't say I'd seen the actual force-field itself. I said that I'd seen it working." she specified. "There's a distinct difference."

"A subtle one, maybe" Maurice compromised. "Alright, how do you know that it's *working* then?"

"Because the cars come to a stop every time, even though you can hear their engines still running. I've never seen one get through yet"

"And how many times have you seen it in action?" probed Maurice, still not without a few misgivings. "It might just have been a coincidence."

"Look Buster" Erin spoke suddenly with a new intensity "That road made an orphan of me. I've no brothers or sisters left either. I'm not about to start taking risks now and end my family bloodline forever, all for a spot of jay-walking. But I'm a hedgehog and hedgehogs cross roads. It's what we do; our *raison d-etre*"

"Oh, I'm so sorry" came Maurice's sombre reply "I didn't realise."

"Of course you didn't. You weren't to know. How could you?" The sudden memories of her lost family seemed to visibly soften Erin right before his eyes and he realised that she could probably be quite pretty if she made the best of herself.

"I can assure you that the force-field works, but you have to get across before the beeping stops and the lights change back to their original darker colour, otherwise it's splat!" she clapped her hands together to emphasise her point. "Why else do you think that I've been here, jumping up and down like a lunatic? It wasn't just for the good of my figure, I can tell you."

"No, I guess not" admitted Maurice, discretely looking her up and down for the first time since their meeting and not doubting her for a second. "But you surely don't really think that you're ever going to reach it, do you? You're not exactly built for jumping" he added, without really thinking the whole statement through properly first.

"And what *exactly* do you mean by that?" Erin bit. Maurice had clearly hit a nerve.

"I mean that you're, erm, I mean, that you don't have, that is to say, erm, your legs..."

"What about my legs?" she shot him an accusatory glare.

"Well.." Maurice was digging himself into a deeper hole with every jabbering, salvation seeking utterance. Once again, he should have known when to keep quiet.

"Yes?" Erin was clearly not going to let him off the hook lightly.

"I mean that frogs....yes, that's it....frogs....they're built for jumping, aren't they? And you certainly don't have legs like a frog" Erin's scowl was immediately replaced with an affectionate, even slightly amorous smile and Maurice breathed a sigh of relief.

"Ooh, you saucy little devil! Flattery will get you everywhere" flirted Erin, fluttering her eyelids outrageously, obviously easily humoured with the simplest of compliments – not that it had actually ever even been intended as one in the first place really. "I do get a lot of comments on my legs you know..."

"I just don't think that you will ever be able to reach the initiator" Maurice went on, undeterred "You don't really think that you can, do you?" His questions were observations rather than criticisms.

"Well, maybe not on my own" she eyed little Maurice "But I might be able to now, with a little help."

"From where?" The penny hadn't dropped. A few seconds. Erin raised an eyebrow, her eyes never leaving his. And then it had. "From me?"

"No stupid, from that big red fox behind you" Maurice spun around, his heart in his mouth, before Erin had a chance to complete her sarcastic retort. "Of course, you!" Maurice did not appreciate the wind-up one little bit. He'd already had enough excitement in the last few days to last his tiny ticker several lifetimes, thank you very much.

"But what can I do? I'm even shorter...I mean, that is to say, I'm not nearly as tall as you."

"On your own, maybe nothing" she admitted "But working together, we'd be significantly taller."

"Oh, I get it" Maurice was beginning to see where this was going. Or at least he thought he was.

"If I stood on your shoulders and you stood on tip-toe, we might be able to reach" she suggested.

This was not at all what Maurice had had in mind. He put forward another suggestion:

"Don't you think it might be better if I were to stand on *your* shoulders instead?"

"Why? What difference does it make? We'd still be the same height." She seemed genuinely confused.

Maurice chose his words carefully "Well, you're a bit more, erm, I mean, I'm probably not as, erm, strong as you. You look ever so toned. Do you work out regularly? Probably all that exercise, jumping up and down, I imagine. I'm just a feeble little mouse" he added, deciding that putting himself down and angling for the sympathy vote might help get her on his side and sway the argument in his favour. He stood upright, touching both forepaws, fists clenched, to his shoulders to demonstrate his lack of biceps, but put them down again quickly, surprised to notice that they seemed a little larger and more defined than normal. There were definite signs of the beginnings of a small bump on each arm. Mouscles! It must have been all that rowing. 'We are Mus Musculus!' he thought to himself, chuffed to bits at his burgeoning more macho physique and quoting The Major's proud catch-phrase.

"Oh, I see" Erin smiled again, finally coming round to his way of thinking. "Yes, well, you're probably right. You do look like you could do with beefing yourself up a bit." She was clearly not prepared to massage Maurice's tender ego in return. He didn't think that the same could be said for her but wisely remained diplomatically silent – something he was rapidly managing to get the hang of. "Come on then, up you get!" The hedgehog leant forwards against the pole, bracing herself ready to take Maurice's full, though insubstantial, bodyweight. He looked unenthusiastically at her thorny, spine-covered back and shoulders and wondered how he was going to do this. Fumbling around awkwardly behind her for a few moments he tried, without luck, to find an appropriate place to start mounting. He hoped nobody would walk past at that particular moment. He couldn't climb up onto her shoulders without being scratched to bits and, as for standing on tip-toe, even if he did manage to get up there, why it would be like standing on a bed of nails. He might still have a long arduous journey ahead of him and couldn't afford to make it on hole-punctured feet. Apart from the obvious physical pain, if it rained, they might leak and cause him to fill up with water. He didn't much relish the prospect of drowning internally from the soles of his feet upwards. No, there had to be some other way. "There must be some other way" he suggested. I'm afraid I'll be cut to ribbons if I try to climb up your back. This just isn't going to happen."

"Well, I did say that I should climb up onto your shoulders" Erin persisted.

"We've already discussed that." Maurice stood firm.

"My underside is much softer. You could climb up my front and onto my chest."

"Is there no other way?" Maurice was reticent.

"No" came Erin's emphatic response, perhaps a little too quickly for his liking.

And so, Maurice set about his awkward search for appropriate places to get a good grip and pulled himself up her tensed, trembling torso.

A few successful manoeuvres later and his feet were off of the ground, wrapped tightly around Erin's waist so that his face was pressed up against hers. Maurice thought what a surreal pairing they would have made at that moment to any passers by who could easily have gotten the wrong idea. At least, he *hoped* that things were not as they appeared. Certainly not as far as he was concerned but, as Erin closed her eyes and parted her lips, Maurice didn't hang around long enough to find out otherwise and clamoured onwards and upwards, onto her chest. Realising, once there, that this position left him even more vulnerable, his mousehood now exposed at face level, he continued climbing, hoping that his tiny, featherweight frame wouldn't be too heavy to bear as he stood on her head, taking care to avoid her crown of thorns. .

"What are you doing up there? This wasn't what we discussed." Erin sounded more disappointed than uncomfortable.

"I know" agreed Maurice "But you want us to reach the initiator, don't you?"

"Oh yes, the initiator" recalled Erin, apparently having completely forgotten what it was that they were even doing there in the first place.

"Now, stand up on tip-toe!" instructed Maurice, masterfully.

"I am" grumbled Erin beneath him.

"Oh! Me too." Maurice was deflated "I'm afraid that we're still nowhere near it."

He couldn't help thinking that there must be a simpler solution and that they were probably making a mountain out of a molehill.

Ray

"What on earth is going on out there!?" came an irate voice from the gardened area behind them. "Will you two cut it out? Some of us are trying to sleep. Do you have any idea what time it is?" the question was rhetorical. In truth, neither of them had the slightest clue, now that he came to mention it.

"No!" they chorused back in unison, and then Maurice added "What time *is* it?", keen to find out. It seemed like a lifetime ago that he'd set off that morning.

"Oh." The voice clearly wasn't expecting an actual answer. "Well, I don't know, but it's late!" He replied abruptly, as if this was as accurate as any speaking clock, before adding as an afterthought "...or early, depending on your point of view"

"I'm terribly sorry sir, but it's not how it looks" explained Maurice, suddenly aware of how ridiculous the two of them, grappling there, must have appeared and sliding down Erin's front, back to terra firma.

"Looks? Well I'm afraid it doesn't *look* like anything to me young man. I'm as blind as a bat, you see. Well actually, no, that's not technically accurate. Bats aren't in fact totally blind. That's a bit of a myth. Angling for the sympathy vote no doubt. They just have incredibly poor eyesight. The little daredevils prefer to use echo-location to navigate" he digressed, as if anyone had asked him in the first place. "I, on the other hand, *am*. Blind, that is. I rely on my more tactile senses for getting around. So you see, and pardon the oversight, I'm actually *blinder* than a bat. So, for me personally, I'm afraid it's not so much how it looks as how it sounds. And I must say, all that huffing and puffing certainly does put ideas in one's head. This is a respectable neighbourhood. Not a single ASBO in the whole village and we'd very much like to keep it that way thank you very much."

"Oh, sorry." Apologised Maurice again "I didn't realise. Well it's not how it *sounds* then."

"What's the story then? And speak up!"

"It's an emergency"

"What sort of emergency?"

"Well, we both need to cross the road you see. I need to get home to my family. My mother will be terribly worried about me. And Erin here...." he gestured in her direction before remembering that the mole was completely blind and, lowered his fore-paws, "Well, she just needs to cross the road too because, well...she has her own reasons."

"Why didn't you say so earlier? Come over here and I'll be happy to help if it means that I can finally get some shut eye without all that commotion going on right on my door-step."

"That's frightfully kind of you sir" thanked Maurice, walking over with Erin to where the mole sat, atop his tiny molehill, resting on his elbows, and getting a better look at him.

His glossy black coat shone with a metallic irridescence, making it appear grey in a certain light. His bleary eyes were so small and squinty that Maurice doubted that he'd have been able to see very much through them anyway, even if he wasn't blind.

"Please, call me Ray. And your name and rank?"

"Sorry, how rude of me. I'm Maurice; erm, housemouse. I think I've already introduced Erin. She's a hedgepig" he replied, oblivious to her scowel, extending his tiny paw to meet the mole's huge six-fingered, powerfully clawed shovel, outstretched before him.

Ray asked how he'd come to arrive there in the first place and Maurice began by telling him all about his foolishly going out where his father had forbidden him to and getting caught in the trap and delivered out to who knew where, way out here in the sticks.

"Hmm" the mole muttered, "Absent without leave eh? Go on."

Maurice told him of all his adventures so far as Ray listened in awe, his lower jaw dropping slowly further open with each new detail. He explained to the mole how mice were considered pests in the town as Ray furiously nodded his understanding. "I know exactly what you mean. Us moles are considered pests too. The expression always makes me laugh" he said, although he wasn't laughing – far from it. "People call virtually every animal they come across 'pests' for one reason or another but they're the only *real* pests. They bulldoze their way into every spare inch of available land without giving so much as a moment's thought to the numerous animal inhabitants and their families who have set up homes there for decades; centuries even. They knock down trees to build motorways, turn huge areas of countryside into agricultural land, combine-harvest the fields, pollute the lakes and rivers with their waste chemicals and the air with their exhaust fumes and smoke and what do they give back? Nothing! They just take, take, take; and they have the cheek to call *us* pests! We were here first. Just because they want a nice neat shag-pile of unblemished grass, am I meant never again to know the glorious feel of fresh, cool air on my face? They put poison and traps down for me too, young man. I've been in one of those humane traps, the same as the one you mentioned. They've even tried flooding and smoking me out; all because of a few small mounds of earth on their blessed lawns. It'll take more than that to get rid of me though. Who do they think they're messing with? I'm not just any old Tom, Dick or Harry. I escaped from a prisoner of war camp. Tunnelled my way out. I was in the Molestream Guards, you know."

And this was Maurice's cue to speak of his father, explaining how he was a military mouse and how he felt that, as a son, he himself had always been a bitter disappointment to him, compared with his older, superior siblings. "I don't think you'll have to worry about that anymore" assured Ray "If all the things you've just told me are true then you've already survived covert operations which I'm sure will rival the best that he has to offer. We just need to get you back home so that you can swap old war stories together." Maurice, playing the scene over vividly in his mind, was smiling so much that his cheeks ached.

"Welcome to Chez Ray!" invited the mole, gesturing towards the crumbling mound of dried soil. "Step right this way!" and with that, he disappeared down the hole. Maurice followed easily after him, dropping down into the pit and experiencing a fleeting, uncomfortable feeling of deja vu, which he attributed to his recent stay in the claustrophobic, lightless trap where all the trouble had started. There was very little light here either, save for the thinnest slivers of silvery moonlight just managing to peek their way down through the hole to the ground below and fading off into the maze of chambers leading away off in every direction. "It's awfully dark" Maurice hesitated.

"I'm afraid it's an underground tunnel and it's night time. What else did you expect? Nice neat rows of fairy-lights illuminating the way, I suppose?" Ray obviously didn't suffer fools gladly; a real, old fashioned, no nonsense mole's mole.

"I don't know" said Maurice, clearly concerned. He thought how ironic his nickname was or, at least, how it sounded. He was certainly no Maurice Miner, that was for sure!

"Well don't you worry your little head about a thing" Ray consoled him "I'll lead the way. I know these tunnels like the back of my claws. Should do; dug most of them myself. Spent my whole life in darkness too. It's really not that bad, once you get used to it"

Maurice hoped he wouldn't have to but was happy nonetheless to be in the company of such a top-class tunneler and hurried forwards to catch up with his new guide, calling urgently after him "Hold on just a second please sir! We need to wait for Erin."

"What the devil is taking her so long?" Ray was becoming impatient. He clearly wanted to get this all over with so that he could get back to his bed as soon as possible.

The two of them returned to the entrance to the chamber, which was now darker than ever. Looking up, they were met with Erin's face suspended from the ceiling of earth above, a few crumbs of soil falling past her ears and down onto them both as she tried, in vain, to squeeze the rest of her body through the tiny hole. She just about managed to wriggle her fore-paws and shoulders through but, being naturally quite pear shaped, her larger midriff and hips were wedged in behind. Maurice jumped up, grasping her paws in an attempt to pull her through but found himself suspended, hanging in the air with his hind feet kicking at nothing and so couldn't get any leverage to assist his plight. Ray in turn pulled at Maurice's tail, leaning back and digging his heels into the ground like an anchorman in a tug-of war. Apart from being rather painful for Maurice, it yielded no other significantly positive results. Maurice thought that she could have benefitted from having spent a little more time exercising in the past. As well as the jumping mentioned previously, her robust physique was obviously not built for pot-holing either. They were in danger of wedging her ever more firmly into the hole until she was stuck fast, rear quarters exposed for any potential passing predator to make an opportunistic meal - or worse – of. At least they wouldn't be short of a tooth-pick once they'd finished. For once, Maurice was glad of his tiny frame.

"This just isn't going to work" conceded the aching hedgehog "You'll pull my arms clean out of their sockets. Just go on without me. Save yourself" she added, placing the back of her paw on her forehead, with all the dramatic over-emphasis of a silent movie starlet, although clearly not really meaning what she said at all.

"I can't just leave you here. We're in this together" stated Maurice.

Erin barely even let him finish his sentence before responding. "Oh well. If you insist. You're very masterful!"

"Look" said Maurice "I'll go ahead with Ray and see if there's anything I can find on the other side which we might be able to use. Maybe I could find a long twig or something which I could bring back with me to press the initiator with."

"We'll never be able to lift a three foot long stick" she slumped.

Maurice was unphased "Well, maybe we could use it to pole-vault ourselves up there instead. We have to try *something*" and with that he set off, after Ray, into the darkness.

The subterranean journey was altogether a wholly unpleasant experience from start to finish, with woodlice curling up like tiny mouse-size footballs as he accidentally kicked them and winding centipedes stepping on his feet a hundred times in return as they scuttled past. At least, he guessed that that's what they were. He couldn't actually see anything for sure. Stumbling around, tripping over loose stones and clods of earth, lurching forward into Ray's silky behind, he bumped his head against snaking fibrous tree roots and nearly had a heart attack at every wriggling invertebrate that he heard or felt pass close by. Every veil of long-uninhabited cobweb which clung to his scrunched-up face conjured up images of multi-eyed, hairy-legged, orange-kneed spiders, lying ravenously in wait at their centre for the smallest dinner-bell vibration, a thick black curtain rendering his vision totally useless. He remembered how terrified he'd been in the plastic trap and tried to imagine how poor Ray managed to live his whole life like this. He never got to see anything, never experienced the wonderful kaleidoscope of colours that the natural world had to offer. He would never view the warm tortoishell hues of a red admiral, fluttering on the air like bouncing petals; would never witness the true crimson beauty of an erupting poppy field, signalling the first advent of spring or know the chime of bluebells in his peripheral vision, demanding recogniton. He would never gaze into the eyes of his own wife, watch his children grow or even see his own arms stretched out before him, just as Maurice hadn't been able to, not so very long ago. A wave of guilt washed over Maurice suddenly as he realised how unjustified his own self-pity had been at just the one single day that he'd spent in darkness. What he *could* see, now, quite clearly, for the first time, was that nobody was really any better than anybody else, that everyone had something to offer, some skill or talent which others might not possess. Ray may be the one without sight up on the surface, but here in the maze-like underground network of tunnels, it was Maurice who was blind. Whilst Ray seemed to swim effortlessly through the earth like a sub-terrapin, he, on the other hand, was awkward, helpless and totally dependant on his retinally challenged ranger if he were ever to make it out again. His eyes were of little use to him down here.

The sudden lack of dangling roots combing at his fur, indicated the beginning of the road above them and then, further on, as they suddenly brushed at his back again, making him recoil in shock, he knew that he must be nearly at the other side. The tunnel sloped upwards, increasingly steep as the faintest outlines of the uneven ground beneath his feet developed into view like a photograph in a dark room, the moonlit hole inviting their welcome exit on the other side. Climbing out and brushing the soil from his tangled fur, Maurice thanked Ray who in turn muttered something about being glad to have been of service but countering it with a grumbling 'no rest for the wicked' and 'you're on your own from here' and something about having to get up early in the morning, as he disappeared off again, leaving the abandoned little mouse unable to get back to help the waiting hedgehog on the opposite side of the street. Maurice wondered if the mole rose religiously early each dawn, in the same way that his own father always did.

Climbing out onto the lawned area, Maurice was surprised to discover just how exact a mirror image of the other side of the road he had arrived at. So much so in fact that, for a minute, he worried that he had just gone around in a huge circle and ended up right back where he started. It wasn't until he noticed the slightly rusted bicycle wheel, tethered upright against the pole which formed the other post of the goal to the village, with an impressively robust-looking, padlocked metal chain, wrapped in clear blue plastic, that he was sure he had successfully made the crossing and swapped sides. What a shame for the poor unsuspecting owner that the rest of the bike hadn't been as securely attached to the front wheel as the chain was. The frame had clearly been removed by some unscrupulous thief, he assumed.

The spokes of the wheel shone in the moonlight like a beckoning ladder. A ladder which might very well take him to within reach of what looked very much like a second initiator. He called across to Erin "Don't worry! I'm going to get you across! Now move yourself over to the edge of the curb! I'm going to activate the forcefield from this side! There's another initiator, I think!" And, with that, he commenced the climb to the top, scaling each spoke like a soldier on an assault course. 'Who needs Mouse Cadets!?' he scoffed to himself, flexing his new-found muscles as he chin-upped onto another rung before stretching upwards for the next.

Finally at the summit, he stood on the flexible black surface , reaching for the white button. Even standing on tip-toe, he was still a fair distance away, but noticed how the air-filled (well, half-filled at least; it had been left there now for some time after all) rubber tyre beneath him had a kind of trampoline-like quality as it yielded and flexed beneath his feet. "I'm going to have to jump for it! Get ready!" he called across, before commencing his count-down from 'Three! Two! One!' and after a few bounces, leapt into the air with all his might, just barely slapping at the protruding white disc with the very tips of his outstretched claws, before plummeting back down the side of the wheel, grabbing desperately at the spokes as he fell in an attempt to slow his descent, so that he came crashing back to the ground with a harmless thud, his pride hurt more than anything else.

As the beeps came, the lights changed colour, just in time to demonstrate the awesome power of the shield at work in all its invisible glory as a large white van pulled up to its edge with a surprised screech, unable to continue on its way.

"Run!" came Maurice's desperate cry, but Erin was in no mood to take orders and had other ideas altogether, basking in her own rare sense of powerful invulnerability. With head held high, she unhurriedly sauntered across the path of the revving vehicle, like a curvy catwalk model, it's headlights bright on her; long, drawn out shadows on the road to her left inflating her so that she appeared huge and important as she held it at bay, the astonished motorist rubbing his eyes with his fists and looking on in disbelief.

Rory

Having said his goodbyes to Erin, following a slightly awkward fairwell thank-you hug which she seemed rather reluctant to let go of, Maurice decided to plough onward. After the shared jubilation at having overcome yet another obstacle, using not just his intellect but, again, his physical strength of all things, he found himself reluctantly alone once more. His mood became more sombre as he had time on his own to contemplate his journey and remind himself of some of the things that he'd seen and heard so far. Whilst the countryside was undeniably beautiful and filled with equally colourful characters that he was quite sure he would never forget for as long as he lived, a life of freedom out in the natural world was not for the faint-hearted and often came at a perilous price. He could not afford to allow his succcessful survival skills thus far to let him become overly confident and careless and so made his mind wander back to some of the wild's stark warnings; there were the two ducklings that hadn't made it back from what should have been a perfectly harmless skinny dip; there was the seemingly invincible Magwitch who, had it not been for a stroke of pure chance and the kind-heartedness and quick thinking of a random passer-by, would surely by now have befallen who knew what awful fate at the hands of his trapper. Horrific, war-like images flooded back into Maurice's head; a plethora of failed pedestrians, kicked to the curb, mere commuter collateral damage to oblivious, indiscriminate mechanical murderers. Dozens of lives meaninglessly lost upon a single road and hundreds, thousands even, of other similar roads just like it, all across the country. And these were just a handful of horror stories, collected from a few encounters in only a couple of days. Doubtless there were countless others being acted out at that very moment in a land not too far away. Life outside was permanently in the balance; a balance which could easily be tipped in fate's favour against any creature, however great or small, wise or wonderful, that didn't keep their wits about them.

A few hours of cautiously battling his way alone through fields of neat rows of crops and occassional tangled undergrowth later, Maurice became aware of the vague outline of a figure struggling towards him in much the same way that he was, only in the opposite direction.

Running low to the ground, neck out-stretched in front of it as if lunging for a finishing line in the hope of a favourable photo-finish decision, and nearing ever closer until finally almost upon each other, the startled bird appeared to see Maurice for the first time, leaping high into the air as it first clapped its wide eyes on him emerging apparently out of nowhere. In fact it would have leapt significantly higher if it hadn't been so conditioned not to do so since birth. Realising relatively quickly that Maurice clearly presented no real physical threat, the puffing, out of breath pheasant stopped to say hello. Or rather it stopped to acknowledge the ever more sociable Maurice's greeting.

"Hello" he said "Going anywhere special?"

"I say young man" answered the bird "You could clear scare a fellow half to death, creeping up on him like that!"

"I'm ever so sorry" apologised Maurice, as usual "I didn't mean to. I was just being polite. If it's any consolation, you startled me too."

"Well of course old bean, of course" harumphed the pheasant "I suppose it is a comfort of sorts, what." He spoke in that way that can be so upper-class that it makes one seem a little eccentric; although, by ornithological classification, a common pheasant, he was anything but. He cut a truly majestic sight, with his long streaked black tail, brightly barred gold and brown body with purple and white markings and bottle green head held regally aloof.

"I'm Maurice" Maurice introduced himself.

"Pleased to make your acquaintance young Maurice" the pheasant offered a wing tip for Maurice to shake. At least, Maurice assumed that that was what he should do. He wouldn't have been at all surprised if the bird had expected him to kneel and kiss it. "Rory Feathers-Whittingbottom" he paused momentarily before adding "the Third" as if this should make all the difference. "Friends call me Rory. Maurice hoped that this category now included himself since they'd formally (well Rory at least; Maurice perhaps not so formally) introduced themselves. He didn't really fancy the idea of having to use the toffee-beaked fellow's full pompous title every time he addressed him.

"So are you then?" reiterated Maurice.

"Am I, what?"

"Going anywhere nice?"

"No" acknowledged the bird "Just keeping on the move, you know. You?"

"I'm just on my way home"

"And where might that be?" enquired the aristocratic pheasant, intrigued to know what such a tiny young figure as this was doing out on his own without any apparent sign of an accompanying responsible adult present, anywhere to be seen.

"Not sure I know sir. I know it's near the coast though".

"Hmm, you'd be best off avoiding the beach, little fellow like you. Liable to get sand kicked in your face, if you ask me" advised Rory.

"I'm not actually planning on going *on* the beach" explained Maurice thinking, with minor irritation that no, he hadn't asked him. He could be a little over-sensitive when it came to references to his size. He'd endured a lifetime, albeit short so far, of derogatory size-ist comments, after all.

"Yes, well, probably just as well" continued Rory, obliviously. "Went there for a day-trip with the family when I was much younger. Didn't get a minute's peace. Blasted seagulls. What an infernal racket! Noisy blighters think they own the damn place."

"Well, they are called *sea* gulls" reminded Maurice, still a little miffed at the indirect reference to his weakling status; particularly since he had only just managed to develop a little pride in what he perceived to be his newly blossoming, more athletic physique.

"Lesser black-backed, actually" parried Rory, a stickler for detail.

"Yes, well anyway" dismissed Maurice " I just hope I'm going the right way, that's all. It's so hard to avoid getting disorientated in these crops. It all looks the same to me in every direction."

"I know what you mean" agreed Rory "I've been going round and round in circles in these here few acres for as long as I can remember."

Maurice wondered why he didn't just fly up into the air to get a good look around, in order to see exactly where he needed to get to. He deduced that Rory must therefore simply be exhibiting the kind of unique educated stupidity and lack of touch with the real world that was so often born out of impeccable breeding; reserved for and never more perfectly demonstrated than by those self-appointed members of the so called upper classes. "So where have you been then?" continued the bird.

Maurice proceeded to tell him of his encounters, finishing up with the story of Erin and the invisible force-field.

"I could've done with your help before now" sniffed Rory "I lost my brother and good lady wife to that infernal road"

That was it. Maurice could not contain his curiosity a moment longer. "I'm terribly sorry sir" he blurted "but would it appear churlish of me to ask why you didn't just *fly* over it?"

"Fly!?" barked Rory "Why, I may just as well stand in the middle of the fast lane of the motorway and play chicken with the oncoming juggernauts, what!"

"Why?" pressed Maurice, his curiosity still far from satisfied.

"Because, young man" opened Rory "as any educated ring-necked pheasant (he preferred using the alternative official name for his kind), such as myself, will tell you, leaving the safety of the ground for the open skies spells almost certain death. Why, I'd be blown to smithereens. I think it's something to do with the increased altitude and the resultant atmospheric pressure. One gets to a certain height and then 'Bang!', there's a loud boom and down one comes in a tattered pile of exploded flesh and feathers. The noise then attracts the hounds which come to finish you off, dragging you to their thunder-stick weilding master who hangs you upside down on hooks until you're decomposed and soft enough to cook and eat. As endings go, it really isn't very pleasant for a pheasant."

This was a convincing argument with some very compelling points. Maurice thought about it for a moment, giving them the necessary due consideration before responding. "But surely it's far more dangerous down here on the ground?"

"Well you're entitled to your opinion, of course" replied Rory, diplomatically, clearly not agreeing but showing his impeccable social pedigree nonetheless "But I've always been taught to 'stay down'."

"Who told you that?" asked Maurice, still keen to get the whole picture.

"My father always taught me and all my friends and family used to do the same."

"Taught? Used to?" quoted Maurice, focusing on Rory's use of the past tense.

"Well yes. I'm afraid that they're no longer with us"

"Who's they?" delved Maurice, still further.

"All of them" revealed Rory.

Maurice was horrified. "Oh, I'm so sorry. What happened to them?" he asked, half expecting to hear of some horrendous group accident in which they had all simultaneously perished.

"Well, gosh, where do I start? Let me see now. Daddy was killed by a stoat, Mummy, bless her dear sweet soul, was taken by a combine harvester and my friends, well, they all met with different but equally unsavoury ends too."

"Such as?" probed Maurice, forgetting the delicacy of the subject for a moment, so keen was he to get all the gory details.

"Well, Alastair, dear sweet fellow, was caught in a section of barbed wire, injured his wing and couldn't escape a hungry fox. Tristan, oh dear dear me. Shocking state of affairs. Most unfortunate. The poor chap was fried by an electric fence, intended to keep horses in their paddock, would you believe?"

Maurice barely could. He was stunned. Speechless in fact. Could Rory not see what, to him, seemed glaringly obvious? Not one of his friends or family had lost their lives as a result of flying. In fact, quite the opposite. It seemed that, in this case, flying really was the safest way to travel. Every feathered friend or family member that the pheasant had mentioned had met their rather untimely fate as a direct result of remaining down on the ground when they didn't actually need to. He pointed this out to the colourful character opposite him, who had momentarily drifted off into his own fond reminiscences of lost loved ones.

"Are you trying to tell me" clarified Rory "that I've spent all my time down here on the ground for nothing?"

Maurice thought very carefully about the most sensitive way to phrase his reply.

Figuring that Rory was educated, since he himself had told him so, Maurice asked him if he would like to hear a poem that he'd learned at mouse school which he thought might go some way to providing a suitably fitting response. Rory, keen to prove his love and appreciation of the arts, confirmed without hesitation that yes, he would indeed

like to hear it; and so Maurice, first clearing his throat
with a small polite cough, recited:

"As I slumber in this place,
The sunlight warm against my face
Shadow of grey cloud furrows my brow

Should I retreat for fear of heat
Which, on fair skin, may smarting burn
Or stay and let the summer take my frown?

Should seasons change and dead leaves fall
As I watch, through misted eyes and breath,
The golden yellows turned to rusty brown

Still comfort could I take in all this
Nature's decay which, as memories 'neath my feet
Covers what once was barren ground."

A brief but pregnant silence followed the reading, which
Maurice punctured with "It's called 'Sunblock'"

"Very nice" harumphed Rory who, despite meaning it, had
to then admit "But I'm not really sure of your point"

"Well, it seems to me that, even if it were true and there
was a chance of something bad happening if you flew,
that's a pretty sad way to live your life. Living in fear of
death and disaster. We all have to go at some point. You
know what they say; the only thing certain in wildlife is

143

death and taxidermy. None of us live forever after all. But you're alive, right here, right now. You've been given wings to fly; you should fly. I'd give anything right now to be able to do the same. I'd have been home days ago if I could. Surely you should enjoy every aspect of your life whilst you're still alive and not waste it worrying about the inevitability of dying, which you can't put off forever or do very much about anyhow. There's a huge world out there, as I'm rapidly discovering with each passing day at the moment. If you only limit yourself to a few square miles when you could go absolutely anywhere, then aren't you just wasting your life and the potential you've been blessed with? Why would you want to hang on so dearly, anyway, to a life which you're not fully living? You owe it to all those who don't have your ability to use it or you abuse it, and you insult them in the process." Maurice finished his sermon by recounting his encounter with Ray in the tunnel, embellishing the story with some detail from his time spent in the trap, and explained how it had showed him that he should never again take the gift of sight for granted. His argument was certainly as strong as, if not stronger than, Rory's.

"But what about my father?" appealed Rory, weakly.

"What about him?" answered Maurice.

"Well, just supposing that he *were* looking down upon me. He'd know that I'd gone against his wishes and everything he taught me. Surely I should stay on my feet out of respect for my father, if nothing else."

144

Maurice knew, all too well, how it felt to want so desperately to gain the respect of a firmly principled father but, at the same time, want to live a life of his own choosing. As an outsider though, it was somehow easier to see things more clearly.

"Looking down on you from *where* exactly?" he asked.

"Well, you know. Figure of speech and all that. Up there." Rory gestured up to the sky with his eyes.

"Up ....*there*?" Maurice looked upwards too in the same way, smiling knowingly. Rory smiled too. It was a sign. Almost as if his father had sent this little rodent as his own personal cherubic mouse messenger.

"You know what?" replied Rory "I think you're right. My father wouldn't have wanted me to live my life in fear, would he? He would have wanted me to enjoy myself and the abilities that I've been blessed with."

"Like flying?" asked Maurice, rhetorically.

"Like flying!" echoed Rory

"So, are you game?" asked Maurice, smiling enthusiastically, keeping the motivational momentum going and whipping him up into a crescendo of courage.

"I most certainly am!" cried Rory, oblivious to the unintentional duplicity of the declaration and, with that, he leapt into the air, flapping his stiff wings properly for the first time in his life, in an effort to propel himself above the tops of the vegetation and into the air. "Look at me Maurice!" he called down "I'm doing it! I'm flying! I'm an aviator! The red, brown and green baron! They'll see me for miles around! The famous grouse; no longer all bottled up, an untethered spirit, free at last!"

"Very impressive!" called back Maurice, with a delighted smile, exaggerating politely at the cured pheasant's rather ungainly yet valiant first attempt.

"You've set me free Maurice. I can see for miles. I wish you could see what I can see from up here."

"I wish I could too!" shouted Maurice "That way I could see where the coast is so I'd know what direction to head in!"

"I can see it" enthused Rory "You're doing just fine. Keep on going the same way in a straight line and you'll come to it eventually!"

"Thank you!" shouted Maurice.

"No" shouted back Rory, getting ever higher as he realised that he wasn't going to burst like a balloon. "Thank *you*!" and he soared off into the distance, watching the tiny speck that was little Maurice, down on the ground, off on the move again already. Grouse in one direction, mouse in the other.

As Maurice pressed onwards, edging ever further away from the scene of his brief but impactful encounter with

Rory, he thought that he made out the barely discernible, muffled 'Boom!' of a single thunder clap, coming from the direction in which he had just been travelling, stifled and softened by both air and distance. Disappointed that he had not witnessed the phenomenal accompanying flash of lightning that usually preceeded it, he looked up into the sky filling the horizon behind him, expecting to see thick black clouds rolling ominously in and was bemused to find it almost completely clear and cloudless. He waited expectantly for a subsequent intermittent lightning bolt or perhaps instead a second grumbling peal of thunder, in order that he might time the gaps between them and gauge whether or not the storm was heading in his direction or moving off to bellow its arrival elsewhere.

But none ever came......

Angus

Maurice had a more spritely spring in his step following his fruitful encounter with Rory. It seemed that he'd developed a new knack for sorting out other creatures' problems. Why was it so much easier to give advice than it was to receive it? This was one dilemma that he didn't have an answer to, which he supposed was exactly the case in point perfectly illustrated really. He didn't know but, either way, it felt good just to be listened to for once – to have a voice of his own which others sat up and took notice of.

The brilliant colours all around him would not have looked out of place on the set of a Bollywood movie; purple heather, bracken and yellow gorse up to his left, bluebells, golden buttercups, snow-white-trimmed daffodils, scarlet red roses and lilac mother's pride to his right. The technicolour surroundings were nearly matched only by Maurice's rouged cheeks, flushed all aglow from the exercise and excitement of his trip. Passing beneath a low wooden fence, he soon stumbled across an abandoned orchard of assorted fruit trees. Half-eaten fallen apples lined the ground as bloated maggots gorged themselves, fuelling up and counting down to launch, ready for the imminent airborn metamorphosis to bluebottle status. An accidental rockery had been formed by the collapsed ruins of a surrounding, ancient dry-stone wall. As Maurice approached it, he stepped through the irregular, crumbled slabs and the rough grass poking through the gaps. Hoisting himself up between the larger cracks, crags and crevices, like some ropeless, adrenalin-seeking free-climber, he was met with the scaley, coiled figure of a slow worm, basking in the warm sun, atop one of the conveniently created flat stone sun patios .

"Hello" said Maurice, braver now with every new encounter and getting quite used to initiating conversations with complete strangers of all species.

"Hello?" questioned the disgruntled looking creature. "Now you're either very brave or very s-s-s-s-stupid" He hissed the beginning of the word 'stupid' in a long, drawn out, exaggerated stutter which, it seemed to Maurice, didn't sound at all natural.

"Oh? Why's that?" asked Maurice, genuinely curious.

"Are you not s-s-s-s-scared of me?" asked the serpentine stranger, somewhat indignantly.

"Scared?" repeated Maurice "Why should I be scared? You're just a s......." But the sudden wounded expression on the little lizard-like face made him hesitate, reluctant to finish his sentence. He knew only too well how it felt to be outcast or ridiculed for not fitting in or being tough enough.

"S-s-s-s-snake. That's-s-s-s right!" he whistled, though due in no part to the contribution of a forked tongue, since there was none present.

"Oh, of course. How silly of me!" offered Maurice, taking pity on the poor disillusioned soul but not wishing to hurt his feelings. "Well, yes, you really do cut quite a frightful figure. Aaaanyway...." he shuffled awkwardly from one foot to another "I'm afraid I really must be on my way now" he added, keen to get a move on and avoid getting himkself into another difficult situation with an unknown quantity, particularly when this new one was quite clearly as barking mad as a bag of howler monkeys.

"You cannot go anywhere, I'm afraid, without first partaking of the Bush of Truth" insisted the slow-worm.

"of which I, Angus, am the s-s-s-sole guardian and distributor"

"The Bush of.....?" Maurice began to repeat, seeking clarity.

"Yes-s-s-s-s" interrupted Angus. "The Bush of Truth"

"Partaking of....?" Maurice wasn't sure what this meant. "I'm afraid I'm not really sure what that means" he said.

"It means" huffed the slow-worm "that you must partake of the Fruit of the Bush of Truth; a berry from its very branches; a Berry of Truth; a Trueberry if you will – before you can be permitted to proceed any further on your Journey of Revelatory Enlightenment"

Maurice was getting really confused by now. Partaking of? Bush of Truth? Journey of Revelatory Enlightenment? He couldn't make sense of some of the elaborate language that was being used. Maybe it was Reptilian? It certainly wasn't a tongue that he was familiar with, forked or otherwise. "I'm really most terribly sorry sir" said Maurice, as respectfully politely as ever "But I honestly don't have the faintest idea what you're talking about!"

"Oh, for goodness sake" said Angus, completely forgetting to emphasise the additional S's at the beginnings and endings of his words momentarily and dispensing altogether with the haunting tone that he'd adopted previously in a vain attempt to add an air of mystery and dramatic emphasis to proceedings. "You can't carry on any further until you've eaten some berries from this bush!" He gestured towards the bush to his right with a movement of his head, since he had no arms or legs with which to do so. The bush looked suspiciously like an everyday common or garden blackberry bush to Maurice.

"But they're just blackberries, aren't they?" he queried.

"Well, I'll grant you that, yes, they do look fairly similar, possessing many of the visual qualities of a plain and simple blackberry. I could even see how, to an untrained eye such as your own, they could indeed perhaps be quite easily mistaken for just such a perfectly ordinary common or garden variety, particularly since they taste remarkably similar too, but I can assure you that, no, they are in fact really most certainly something quite altogether different."

"Oh" replied Maurice, unconvinced "I see" But he didn't really see at all. If his journey had taught him anything though, it was perhaps that it was sometimes kinder to agree with somebody, even when you didn't, than upset them with the making of an unproductive point. "So I just have to eat a single bla...... I mean, Berry of Truth, and I can be on my way?"

"Yes-s-s-s" hissed Angus once more, remembering all of a sudden to get back into cobra-esque character.

"Ok" said Maurice, with a mock gesture of resigned trepidation "Here goes!" and he plucked down one of the biggest, blackest, juiciest looking berries that he could find, taking care to avoid scratching himself on the surrounding thorns as he did so. Opening his mouth as far as it would stretch, he took a huge (well at least for a mouse, anyway) bite. To be honest with you, he was quite glad of the opportunity to get some food inside him at last. Chewing exaggeratedly for dramatic effect, the rich sugary juice bursting forth, running down and soothing his parched little throat, he disguised his appreciation with a pretend grimace as he swallowed, almost giving himself away at the end of the performance with a contented, smack of the lips and open-mouthed sigh but cleverly, at the last minute, turning it instead into a disgusted facial expression, sticking his tongue out as if wretching and gagging. He wanted Angus to believe that he had just undergone an excruciatingly unpleasant ordeal, rather than the converse reality, which was that he had in fact just enjoyed a much needed sweet and succulent snack; it wasn't exactly Battenberg admittedly, but it wasn't too bad. Not too bad at all. Organic too; his father would be proud. He felt that the slow-worm would probably be more satisfied with this too somehow and hence allow him to pass, content in the knowledge that the mouse had made some kind of spiritual sacrifice and earned his rite of passage. The whole while that this was happening, a transfixed Angus had watched in morbid fascination, half wondering if the berries might actually be poisonous; his head bobbing up, down and around, in time with each sideways chewing movement of Maurice's mousticating jaws.

"Well?" he asked, at last, desperate to know if it had actually worked. Unbeknown to Maurice, this was the first time that anyone had ever done as Angus had asked and sampled the seasonal special. "Can you feel anything?"

"Absolutely!" enthused Maurice, hamming it up with such theatrical aplomb that he was in grave danger of giving the entire game away before he'd even managed to get Angus to play along as planned. "It's really quite amazing. I can see the truth in almost everything. Ask me anything and I'll try to lie! I'll bet you I couldn't, even if I tried. It makes you look right inside and see yourself for who and what you really are. It lets you see the mistakes that you might have made in the past. It's an epiphany!" Maurice was spurred proudly on by his long word, glad of the opportunity to use it: and in context too!

"Like what? What can you see then?" urged Angus, keen for some hard and fast examples to substantiate Maurice's revelatory claims.

"Well, like for instance, that you shouldn't try to be something that you're not. You should learn to be happy with who you are; that you can't expect others to love you, or even like you come to that, unless you're content from within first and accepting of your, after all, inescapable lot. Take my father, for example. Please!" Maurice laughed, lightening the lecture "He has always wanted me to be a mouse of action but I've always been more a mouse of words; a thinker rather than a doer. In all honesty, I'd rather read a good book or play chess than sports. My idea of a good play is 'The Taming of the Shrew'! I think I've always known, deep down, that I'm a bit of a disappointment to my dad but the berry has shown me that I shouldn't worry what others, including him, think so much. If I just stay true to myself then the rest should all work itself out in the end. And if it doesn't, well at least I can live with myself and love myself, even if he doesn't."

"That's unbelieveable" said Angus, believing every word and forgetting his sporadic hoax hisses again. "All that from just one berry! Just imagine what you'd get if you ate the whole bush-full!"

'A terrible tummy ache' thought Maurice, cynically, although he opted instead for a few compromising concordant coos of "Absolutely!" and "Just imagine!" And somehow he wasn't lying. Not really. Maybe it hadn't worked for the reasons that Angus had originally intended, but eating the berry had simply allowed Maurice a rare moment's inward reflection which, in turn, had been all the placebo that he'd really needed to enable him to look at his own situation so objectively. If it could do this for him, when he didn't even really believe that the berry had any magical powers whatsoever, then imagine indeed what it might do for someone else who had faith that it would work. "You should try one!" he suggested.

"Oh I don't know" came Angus's reticent reply.

"Come on! I did it. What are you so afraid of?" Maurice wasn't too principled to resort to a little emotional blackmail when circumstances required it.

"I'm not afraid of anything" came Angus's rapid-fire response "In fact, anything is afraid of me!" It was an unconvincing show of bravado.

"Well go ahead then! You might be surprised at what you discover"

After a little time spent pondering the possible ramifications and plucking up the necessary courage, Angus took the tiniest, most miniscule nibble of one of the smallest berries, within easy reach, that he could see. The result was that he chose a relatively unripened one, still a little green in places. He winced at the sharp taste and cunning little Maurice seized the chance to deliberately misconstrue what this meant.

"Same thing happened to me" he said. "Hits you right between the eyes, doesn't it? I can see from your face that you feel it working already."

"Yes-s-s" answered Angus, reverting to fake-snake speak. He wasn't kidding either. He had pretty much convinced himself, with more than a little gentle, cajoling persuasion from Maurice, that the power of the berry was genuinely taking effect. "I think I do feel something."

"It's worked!" exclaimed Maurice, clapping his paws together "You even look different. Why, I never saw a more honest face; truly I didn't!"

"Try it then! Ask me a question!" demanded the deluded taste-tester.

"Ok then" Maurice thought carefully for a few minutes; or at least, he pretended to. The crafty little thespian had actually already decided on a question, long before Angus had even asked him.

"What sort of snake are you, exactly?"

Angus's lipless smile dissipated immediately "Why did you ask me that?" he stalled, avoiding answering the question directly at first.

"Well" explained Maurice "You don't look much like a grass snake, smooth snake or adder to me and as far as I'm aware, they're the only three kinds of snake native to this country" (I'm sure it will come as no surprise to the reader to discover that Maurice had always paid avid attention during Natural History lessons at school. Turns out Mr Genus was right about education never being a waste after all). "And most snakes usually eat mice too but I'm a mouse and you're actually really rather nice and friendly. So either you're a foreign....."

"I'm a British citizen, born and bred, I'll have you know!" came Angus's rapid ripost. He seemed deeply offended, almost to the point of mortification, at the mere suggestion that his patriality might be called into question.

"..and, well, you're .... pink!" Maurice soldiered on.

"And what *exactly* is that supposed to mean? What are you trying to accuse me of?" Angus flushed with indignation, ironically resulting in an even more pronounced hue of the pigment that he believed to be under attack in the first place. He was unnecessarily defensive though, for Maurice was merely making a colourful observation and not judging or defaming him in any way whatever. So he told him so.

"Nothing" he said "Nothing at all. I like pink. In fact, it's one of my favourite colours .... along with yellow" his mind wandered momentarily and he gulped down a mouthful of saliva which had formed a small pool around his tiny tongue.

"So is this line of questioning leading anywhere?" interjected Angus, preparing to raise another objection which self-appointed judge Maurice would no doubt take it upon himself to overrule again.

"Well yes, to my point of course...."

"Which is?"

"Which is ..... that if you're not foreign and you're not a grass snake, smooth snake or an adder, then ....." Maurice trailed off.

"Then, what?" challenged Angus, becoming impatient for the elusive point which, perversely, part of him didn't want made in the first place, for fear of being forced to acknowledge its validity.

"I don't know. It just doesn't seem to make any sense to me" answered Maurice, telling the truth, berry or no berry; for it certainly didn't.

The slow-worm took a deep, reticent breath, as if holding back what he was about to say, before deciding with a potentially relief inducing resignation that maybe he should just go ahead anyway, his tongue oiled by the lubricating fruit juice of truth now flowing through his long, gurgling small intestine. "Can I let you into a little s......secret?" he said, finally; he started to hiss the beginning of the word 'secret' but paused, thought better of it and then said it normally.

"Please do" encouraged Maurice "I promise you, I'm very trustworthy and discrete. It won't go any further. You have my word."

"It's only the berry which has revealed this to me, you understand?"

"Of course" replied Maurice, understanding perfectly.

"I'm not, *technically*, a real snake" he divulged.

"You're not!?" Maurice reacted with an admirable expression of unbridled astonishment, keeping up the histrionic pretence. "What are you then?" He needed it to come from Angus himself.

" Well, I *am* a reptile and snakes *are* reptiles" he justified. "So I'm sort of .... *almost* ...... *nearly*..... a snake. Same family really."

"A distant cousin?" offered Maurice, throwing him a life-line.

"Once or twice removed, perhaps" confessed Angus "I'm a slow-worm. But I'm not really a worm either. I'm actually a type of lizard. I just don't have any legs like a normal lizard. I'm not even slow. In fact, quite the opposite. I can wriggle like greased lightening when the need arises, when my stone gets upturned. So hopefully you can understand why I've been the victim of something of an identity crisis?"

"Definitely" admitted Maurice, who had already tried to put himself into Angus's unfooted shoes and imagine the hurdles that probably came with lacking any real limbs to speak of, being called a slow-worm when you were neither slow nor a worm and, to top it all, a pink one to boot . "Well I, for one, am glad."

"Glad? Why?" asked Angus

"Well, if you were really a snake, then you'd probably have eaten me by now" chortled Maurice.

"Oh yes" Angus chuckled, his shoulders would have been shaking up and down if he'd had any "Well I can assure you that you're really quite safe on that score. The most I can ever usually manage at a single sitting is barely more than a few dozen ants. If I'd eaten you then, apart from a serious case of indigestion, we'd never have had the chance to talk, I'd never have tasted the Berry of Truth and I'd still be living a lie. In the past, I've scared away everyone I've ever met because I was ashamed of who I was and it was easier to attribute my simple solitary existence to that but that's all going to change from now on."

"It might very well be easier to push others away than risk finding out that they just don't like you for who you really are" agreed Maurice "But it's taking those risks that makes the rewards worthwhile. You can't expect *everyone* to like you, but if things don't come at a price, then how can you ever know what they're really worth?"

"You really think so?" asked Angus, seeking reassurance.

"Absolutely!" assured Maurice, as much to himself as to Angus.

"You really think that I could start to make some friends of my own?"

"Well, put it this way" answered Maurice "You've already made one, haven't you?"

Out of the woods

Some hours had passed since having watched a grinning Angus slithering off to find another warm, sunny spot among the rocks and, coming to the edge of the wood, Maurice was struck by the beauty of the sight laid out below. The outer woodland border was at the top of a steep escarpment, allowing him a bird's eye view of the whole landscape. The feeling of elation at finding his way back to a town, hopefully *his* town, along with the acknowledgement of his actual physical position, left him feeling, quite literally, on top of the world. Off in the distance, the hazy glow of static orange lights hummed whilst pink and white dots moved in neat geometrical rows among them, replacing the previously visible swirling milky way of stars twinkling in the night sky above. The reverberation of far off exhaust notes droned up to him on the soft sea breeze, accompanied by the distinctive briney bouquet of mud and salt, blowing in from the coast. The shingly beach snaked along the periphery of his view, separating the bejewelled, bustling city from the dark open expanse of shimmering, moonlit water to his right and Maurice knew that he must be heading in the right direction and that, from the look of things, it was mostly downhill from here. He skipped gaily down the slope, the sharp gradient occassionally building up more momentum than his limited balance was able to contain, as he tumbled and turned in small forward rolls, landing in a chuckling, out-of-breath heap, slowed by the numerous elevated bumps and clumps of tall grass in the uneven ground.

Town

Coming into the busy town centre so soon after his escape to the country supplied a sensory overload, leaving Maurice disorientated by the barrage of artificial sights and sounds. He decided to remain out of view of people as much as possible, just as his father had always taught him. This was easier said than done though. The high street was brightly lit by neon tube lights advertising adult book shops and seedy nightclubs. Gawdy laminated posters hung from lone remaining strips of stubborn, slowly unpeeling sticky tape, boasting of fried chicken meals at bargain prices and generously promising free soft drinks and french fries to those who chose to 'Go Large!'. Flourescent strip lighting and huge plate-glass windows revealed veritable tree-trunks of meat; elephantine amputations rotating slowly against glowing orange heat elements. The roads themselves were filled with the claxon of car horns singing Dixie and the deafening collective din of dozens of hatch-backs with oversized, dustbin-diameter exhaust pipes, deliberately amplified much louder than they were originally intended to be, as thumping bass sounds reverberated in Maurice's sensitive ears from the revving vehicles and many of the late-night establishments which he scurried hurriedly past. The pungent cocktail of cigarettes, alcohol, cheap aftershave and duty-free perfume combined with a nasal onslaught of garlic, chilli sauce and chip fat, seeping out onto the pavements which themselves were amok with marauding packs of jeering, cheering, football-shirted teenagers, stumbling in huddled groups, arms draped around each other to steady themselves as they weaved their way home, warbling untunefully all the way. In a funny sort of way, Maurice thought how the place somehow still had something valuable to offer – a rich, cacophonic kaleidoscopic mix of sights, smells and sounds and a unique wildlife all of its own – just like the wooded areas which he had so successfully managed to traverse over the past couple of days. As he took all of this in, letting his concentration lapse for merely the briefest of moments, a stockily built, brindle-coated bull-terrier spotted him, sounding the alarm for all to hear with its ferocious combination of bronchial barks and salivating snarls through growling, gritted teeth, its long, almost equine nose curled up in a contemptuous, hateful sneer. The dog's desperate lunges were foiled only by the thick metal chain, tethering him to the railing behind, which snapped taut at his studded-collared throat, causing the frustrated canine to jerk back suddenly, yelping in pain just inches from where the wide-eyed house-mouse stood. It was a stark reality check. He wasn't home safe yet. Not by a long chalk.

The Alley

Maurice needed no more persuasion than this to get off of the main thoroughfare and remain out of harm's way. He shimmied along the remainder of the brick wall, keeping his body closely flattened to it to enable him to stay just beyond reach of the yapping brute's still snapping leash and jaws, before ducking down an alleyway which ran between a gentleman's club, decorated with the garish outlines of neon pink and blue dancing girls and musical instruments indicating an underground bassment jazz club, from which came the soothing muted serenade of a saxophone playing the blues. The alley was heavily shadowed and littered with large, overflowing industrial waste bins on black plastic wheels, a moth-eaten, green velour armchair, a stain-speckled mattress which looked like it had seen better days (it had probably belonged to one of the annexing venues) as springs erupted from the stripey material covering and all manner of assorted, discarded waste items, blocking the various fire-exit doors, accessed by a few stone-steps, staggered evenly along the walls on either side. The brickwork was still dark and damp in a number of places, with some unidentified fluid which appeared to have leaked down it from a few feet above ground, about waste-high to a human, forming small frothy puddles at their base and attracting flies and mosquitoes. Maurice made sure to step carefully around these wee pools, not wishing to get his feet wet.

About halfway along the alley, Maurice ceased his nervous whistling as he started to get the feeling that he wasn't alone. He thought that he detected signs of silhouetted movement up ahead and made out the surreptitious hiss of stifled whispers. Pausing to get a better listen, he became instinctively aware of a presence looming behind him. It wasn't even so much that he necessarily saw or heard anything specifically. He just sort of sensed that something was amiss, in that intuitive way that one does sometimes. The mouse equivalent of Spidey sense, I suppose; Mousey sense, if you like, or whatever name you think might better suit it.

A large black rat stepped out of the shadows in front of him, staring at Maurice with a complete lack of expression, all the more sinister for the ambiguous lack of overt aggression, almost as if he had no feelings at all and might therefore be capable of anything. Even in the foreboding circumstances, Maurice wondered fleetingly if this came naturally or if the rat consciously practised the look to intimidate others. Either way, it worked very effectively, and Maurice instinctively turned as if to run, only to find his path back to the road blocked by two more of the same, intimidating looking figures.

"Going somewhere, brother?" asked one of them; not so much a question as a statement of their intent to keep him from going anywhere at all. The question made Maurice wish that his own, real brothers were around right now. This rat too had the same lazy, unblinking gaze as the first, eyelids only half open somehow. Maurice noticed that part of his right ear was missing too, adding to his hard-rat image. His accomplice let out a snigger, as if the very idea of Maurice going anywhere was laughable.

"Nah, he aint goin' nowhere" answered the other, on Maurice's behalf.

"So they got the young 'uns doing their dirty work now then, have they?" came the question from the largest rat; the one that had first blocked Maurice's path. "Too scared to come on their own no doubt, after the whupping we gave them last time." The other two nodded their fervent affirmation.

"Who? What dirty work?" Maurice was genuinely perplexed.

"Don't play the innocent with me!"

"No, really. I'm afraid I don't know what you mean."

"Your lot, of course" came the reply "The brown rats. From over the East side of the alley. Who else did you think we meant?"

"But I'm not a brown rat" appealed Maurice.

"Well what colour are you then? You certainly ain't black like us."

"Well just because I'm not black, that doesn't automatically make me brown, does it?" reasoned Maurice "I mean, there are lots of different colours; and even more hues and shades within those colours. I'm not brown *or* black. I'm somewhere in between. I'm sort of a mixture of browny grey; mousey, I guess you could call it. And just for the record, since you mentioned it, I'm not even a rat!" He wasn't sure if this last detail would endear him to them more and gain him some favour or go against him and make things worse but it was too late to take it back now that it was out there in the open.

"Well, what are you then? You sure look just like a little rat to me"

"Look!" instructed Maurice firmly, lifting his pathetic little tail, as slim as a shoe-lace "Does this look anything like any of yours?"

All three of them simultaneously looked over their shoulders at their own, significantly more substantial, girthy, hairless pink appendages, before collectively agreeing "Well, no, not really"

"Exactly! That's because I'm a mouse" explained Maurice. "For goodness sake! Do you lot *never* leave this alleyway? Admittedly, I do look a bit like a small rat, but that's because I'm a rodent, just like you; and more importantly, just like the brown rats too. You see, we're all part of one big family and families are supposed to stick together, aren't they?"

The three figures shuffled their feet awkwardly, looking intently at the ground, as if searching for the answer; or at least a suitable alternative to the correct one which they probably already knew deep down. Whilst they were on the back foot, Maurice seized the moment to keep the dialogue flowing, in an attempt to ingratiate himself with them further and so perhaps reduce the likelihood of his being set upon.

"I'm Maurice" he announced, in mock-bold self-confidence, offering his tiny pink digits for one of them to take.

The largest rat, clearly the group leader, was so taken aback by the audacious gesture that, without even thinking, he returned it immediately. "Erm, Clay" he introduced himself "This here's Vander" he said, nodding towards his ear-chewed companion.

"Vandal?" Maurice hadn't heard clearly and leant in a little closer, cupping his ear for confirmation.

"No" chuckled Clay "But you're not far off. And that" he said, indicating the last of the grubby looking strangers "That there's Sugar-Ray."

"Oh, is that your real name?" asked Maurice, intrigued.

"No" interjected Vander, huffing, as if it should have been obvious "It's just on account of his sweet tooth"

Sugar-Ray revealed a goofy, yellowish-orange smile which told Maurice that he had obviously never been made to follow the strict, nightly dental regime that he himself had been subjected to. For the first time in his life, he was glad of his father's persistence, although his happiness was immediately tinged with a slight sadness at the parallel realisation that this poor, decay-ridden fellow had obviously never had a father around who cared enough to stop such blatantly apparent oral neglect. He beamed back a sparkling, Colgate smile, all the more visible for its being the only bit of lightness visible in the dense shadows. Maurice thought that he saw a look of embarrassed envy cross Sugar-Ray's face as the rat pursed his lips in an attempt to conceal his own inferior fangs. This only had the effect of turning his smile into more of a grimace though and somehow helped tip the balance of power more in Maurice's favour.

"I have a sweet tooth myself" said Maurice, glad of the opportunity to find something which he had in common with at least one of them so that he could make friendly conversation. This also allowed him to stall for valuable time whilst he gauged the still far from comfortable situation. "Battenberg's my favourite" he added "What's yours?"

"Ooh, I am rather partial to a nice bit of Batty myself" cooed Sugar-Ray "You just can't beat it sometimes. But my favourite? Hmm, now that's a tricky one."

"I can't believe it" squealed Maurice "I call it Batty too. What are the chances?"

"He likes Fairy Cakes" said Vander, grinning sardonically and looking furtively to Clay for support, who instead merely shot him a fierce, disapproving glance. Sugar-Ray was still deep in thought, looking up to the stars for inspiration.

"Fruit!" he squealed suddenly "I do like a nice hunk of fruit cake when I can get my paws on one." Sugar-Ray was clearly enjoying the novelty of having a fellow fudge fancier with whom to share his enthusiasm for confectionery and discuss preferences, for once. Mmm, fudge. His mind wandered momentarily, engrossed in a sudden idea for a new chocolate-related product; five fingers of fudge – 'The Fist'! Or perhaps a five-fingered Kit-Kat of the same name. He knew that Nestle had expanded their range extensively over recent years, to now include 'Minis' and 'Chunkys' among other things. Why, he had a vague recollection that they had even introduced an orange and a peanut-butter flavoured variety at some point, as well as mint, dark and white; so maybe they might just be interested in a concept which could once again encourage renewed interest in their brand. Just think of the potential for headline-grabbing marketing slogans! The possibilities were endless. He was sure that it would attract public attention for one reason or another. It was at times like this that he really wished that he could squeak human. "Although, no, hold on a minute! A lovely chocolate eclair! There's really nothing better" he blurted, coming back to the conversation finally, the previous ideas leaving his head almost immediately, unlikely ever to return again.

"Ooh yes, oozing with real fresh cream!" gushed Maurice. He had gotten so used to having to keep his obsession quiet at home, that being able to come out and rave about his preferences openly in this way with another fellow of the same persuasion was like a breath of fresh air for him too.

Vander was clearly suitably unimpressed by this new friendship being forged right before his eyes when all that he really looked like he wanted, was a good fight. "Enough of all this sweet talk. I say we just teach him a lesson." His tone was gravelly and raw, his teaching credentials highly questionable. He didn't seem the type to have ever *attended* a lesson, thought Maurice, let alone deliver one himself. Maurice reckoned that he'd probably learned everything he knew on the streets, at the school of hard knocks.

"I want nothing more than to learn" parried Maurice, interpreting him literally, in a clever attempt to diffuse the potentially volatile situation and throw his aggressor off balance. At my school, I'm in the top set in all my classes. Except for PE."

Vander's eyes narrowed. "Are you trying to be clever?" he accused.

"Well yes" confirmed Maurice, taking him at his word and disarming him once again. He realised that he wasn't in the school playground now and couldn't rely on the fact that he had older brothers to use as a physical deterrent. "Absolutely. Isn't that the whole point of learning?" The point of facetiousness had now long been and gone.

Vander paused, really genuinely confused now and unsure of whether the little mouse was mocking him or simply meaning what he said "Right, that's it" he said, finally deciding on the former (mainly because the latter would have meant no fighting) and clenching his fists.

"No, wait!" ordered Clay. "They do say that knowledge is power. Let's see what the little squirt has to say for himself. Now, what makes you such an expert?"

"An expert on what?" Maurice's tone was intentionally modest and innocent.

"This rodent stuff you mentioned. Tell me more!" insisted Clay.

"Yeah, we're all ears" said Vander, sarcastically. Maurice stole a glance at the rat's tattered left ear and raised a doubtful eyebrow, making sure that his adversary saw it, safe in the knowledge that Clay would not yet let him come to any harm. Vander said nothing but wasn't good at hiding his feelings and was obviously seething beneath the surface at the little pip-squeak's gumption.

"Well, I read a lot so I know a lot of facts, from books mostly, but I've also experienced a lot for myself now over the last few days and I know that there are lots of different creatures in the world but that 'different' doesn't have to mean 'bad'." He went on to describe all the scrapes that he had managed to get himself into and out of and all the wonders of life that he had witnessed along the way.

"Blimey. We should call you Mighty Mouse" suggested Sugar-Ray

"I think you'll find that that title's already taken" countered Maurice.

"Okay, well how about Danger Mouse then?" he submitted.

"That too, I'm afraid" said Maurice, reluctantly.

"Mini-Mouse, more like it" scoffed Vander "Look at the size of the little runt!"

"Are you taking the mickey?" bristled Maurice, growing in confidence. He mentioned Brody, explaining that he too was another kind of rodent and described how they had managed to overcome a much more powerful adversary by working together, as a team. "So you see, variety is a good thing. It's what gives us our identity and, like my mum always says, it's what makes life interesting. It'd be a boring world if we were all the same. None of us are perfect but it's our imperfections that set us apart from others and make us perfect for someone."

"Go on" encouraged Clay. The other two had stopped squabbling long enough to become interested in Maurice's monologue and were listening intently, fascinated by this puny prophet's pearls of wisdom.

"Sugar-Ray" Maurice continued, addressing his new friend "Would you rather have a single bar of plain milk chocolate or a box of assorted soft-centres?"

"Why, I'd rather have the selection pack of course" enthused his comrade in arms, his childlike attention span already drifting off to thoughts of the imaginary contents.

"Ok, then. Well, there you have it." Maurice naively felt that this should be enough to illustrate his point. He was mistaken.

"I'm not sure I'm with you" confessed Sugar-Ray "I don't usually like all of them though. I'm not a huge fan of the coffee-creams or the hazelnut whirls."

"No, but maybe they're Vander's or Clay's favourites and they could leave the Turkish delight or the clotted fudge for you, so that everyone's happy."

Sugar-Ray and Vander still looked a little unsure, although Clay's frown was noticeably subsiding. It didn't seem to matter to him that he didn't like coffee-creams or hazelnut whirls either. He had to admit it; this little mouse was starting to make sense.

"Ok, well let me put it another way" sighed Maurice, turning again to Sugar-Ray "You love a nice bit of fruit cake. It's one of your favourites, right?"

"Yes" he agreed, readily, almost as if half-expecting Maurice to magically conjur up a huge portion of the baked bounty for him, right there and then, from out of thin air.

"But would you *really* want to eat fruit-cake every day for the rest of your life? Wouldn't you rather know that you could also savour the delights of a firm and crunchy gingerbread-man, a paw-full of chocolate fingers or a custard tart with a side-order of butterscotch?"

"Well of course" a salivating, Sugar-Ray licked his lips "But..."

"But what?"

"Erm... well, nothing, I suppose."

"What I'm trying to show you, is that variety is good. The spice of life in fact, to coin a phrase." Maurice arrived back at his opening statement, wondering where the phrase 'to coin a phrase' came from and what it meant; he made a mental note to look it up, if and when he made it home. The three rats were speechless for once. Their six eyes sought skyward for the understanding and elightenment that their subconscious minds had already discovered. Deep down, they knew that he was right and that somehow it had something to do with their own situation with the brown rats.

"I don't even like cake" was all the obtuse Vander could manage, in his deliberately dismissive way, either completely missing the point or obstinately refusing to accept it on principle.

"So you really weren't sent by the brown rats to spy on us then?" Ever suspicious, Clay still felt the need to double-check one last time

"No. Honestly. I've never even met them. But, just out of interest, what have you got against them anyway?"

"Well they're dirty vermin for one thing" affirmed Vander, quick to respond.

"Yes, absolutely no attention to personal hygeine" Sugar-Ray backed him up, smiling a nervous plaque-coated smile; but his derogatory tone lacked conviction.

"Carry disease" added Vander, scrabbling for reasons.

"The plague." Clay confirmed, barely opening his mouth and nodding almost only to himself.

"I think you may have your historical facts a little wrong." Maurice suggested diplomatically, without elaborating on the point too much at this stage, not wishing to offend them now that he seemed to have been doing so well. "Did you know that people keep brown rats as pets?"

"So?" replied the trio, all at once.

"Well, they wouldn't do that if they were really as dirty as you say, would they?"

"What a load of nonsense" claimed Vander. "Humans are only interested in killing or eating animals. Everyone knows that."

"Well I'm afraid that that's simply not true of all of them." Maurice contradicted "I was caught alive by a human, who drove me out into the country and set me free. He could easily have killed me but chose instead to spare me. He used a humane trap. They're not called *human*e for nothing. So you see, I'm living, breathing proof that some people do care about animals"

This was first hand information, straight from the mouse's mouth, facts that simply could not be denied or refuted as idle gossip or inaccurate rumour. The three scruffy stooges huddled together, conflabbing heatedly, whilst Maurice stood waiting, a furry flanker on the periphery of their mini-scrum. He thought that he overheard Vander appealing to the others about 'not wanting to be seen as no Uncle Tom' and he wondered how the rat had known the name of his human captor; he felt quite sure that he hadn't mentioned it.

"Just go!" Clay told Maurice, breaking away from the group "Before I change my mind."

"You're not *seriously* going to let him go?" appealed Vander, dumbfounded; he was still eager for a little game of his own brand of rat and mouse.

"I most certainly am" Clay was effortlessly emphatic "You've had a lucky escape, little fella". He nodded upwards at Maurice, signalling for him to get moving. Maurice was smart enough to take his cue and didn't hang around, taking care to look as relaxed as possible as he strolled off in his original direction, down the alley, every bone in his body fighting the instinctive urge to run, for fear that he might look guilty of something, giving them cause for second-thought and perhaps provoking a chase. He needed to conserve his energy. He knew that he still had to get past the brown rats yet. Behind him, Vander was undeterred with his desperate appeal.

"But he'll give them valuable information"

"Hopefully" mused Clay, calm and unflinching as ever "Hopefully."

Round 2

Before long, a little further on and a little more confident that Vander's pleas had finally fallen on deaf ears, Maurice's other senses came back into play, overriding the raw survival instinct that he'd been functioning on since taking his leave of the black rats. He allowed himself the luxury of taking in his surroundings for the first time since entering the alley, dank and depressing though they were, with a newly heightened clarity. He stole past solid steel fire doors daubed in scribbles of graffiti; words which he had never learned in class and most likely never would; at least not from his teachers. A coal bunker spilled its dusty residue out onto the concrete, staining the stagnant pools of stale, leaked beer into miniature oil slicks, matted-winged bluebottles washed up on their tideless shores. Plastic crates of empty bottles offered creatures of the night temporary refuge with ribbons of browning lettuce coated in congealed tartare sauce tumbling from upturned styrofoam burger-boxes, providing a room-service midnight feast for the less discerning guest. Sheets of three-day-old newspapers were blown to and fro by the alley-channelled evening thermals, landing on more rubbish, upon yet more paper, creating a lasagne of litter. Cigarette butts and flattened grey discs of de-flavoured chewing gum dappled every square foot of ground whilst half-torn-away Rizla packets looked on. Maurice's hunger for words saw him decipher the message 'Smoking Kills' on the side of an empty card carton and he wondered if this was a reference to the same danger as the 'smoking out' that Ray had referred to previously. He also wondered if the owner of the lone shoe, left standing footless by itself at the base of a tall, suspended fire-escape ladder, had hopped home on the night that they'd lost it. Or perhaps they'd never made it home at all. Ever. The thought sent a shiver through Maurice's already chilly body and reminded him why it was that he needed to keep urgently pressing on; something that he would be required to clarify again, all too soon, as the inevitable happened.

"And where do you think you're off to?" asked the formidably well-built brown rat, stepping out from among a cluster of crumpled black bin-liners, spilling over with rotten food waste. This time, Maurice wasn't nearly as startled as he had been earlier on. He'd been expecting a meeting of sorts to be imposed upon him at some point and even the opening approach was similar to that which he'd already played out in his head. Well, he'd had some experience of this type of situation now after all.

183

"Just home" he answered, keeping things simple to avoid any misinterpretation or inadvertently saying the wrong thing, as two more unsavoury looking brown rats stepped out from among the refuse, flanking their spokesrat.

"Well, seems to me, *homes,* that you're going the wrong way then, innit" the rat replied, laughing humourlessly. "I must say, it comes to something when they send the kids on their secret missions, innit" His two gorillas nodded slowly, eyes closed in an all-knowing kind of way. Maurice couldn't quite understand from his strange use of language whether the rat was asking a question which needed a response, or merely making a statement. He assumed that it must be a type of unique brown rat dialect which he had never come across before. "I suppose I can't blame them. Probably afraid to face us again themselves after our last encounter, innit. Reckon they think we'll go easier on the little'uns." The other two rats with him shook their heads slowly from side to side to indicate that this would most definitely not be the case, eyelids closed again in a slow blink for dramatic emphasis.

"Eh?" reacted Maurice, confused for only a millisecond before the realisation of a re-run hit "Oh, no. Look, before you say anything, I'm not a black rat and I know, I'm not brown either but neither am I a rat at all. I'm Maurice. I'm a mouse. A house-mouse to be precise, which means that I belong at home, in a house. That's where I'm heading right now and have been doing so for the past two days. If you're planning on doing the whole tough guy thing then you can save your breath. I've just had the whole routine from the black rats. They thought I was a brown rat and gave me a hard time for it. For what it's worth, I stuck up for you."

"Oh, really? A house-mouse eh?" asked the lead rat, sceptically. "Well what exactly did you say about us then, *homey*? You don't even know us."

"Yeah" chimed in one of the henchrats "And how come they just let you go if they thought you were on our side?"

"I say he's lieing" suggested the other "Let's just sort him out. Fix him real good."

Maurice responded by confirming that his predicament certainly did need sorting out and that any offer of help fixing it would be greatly appreciated. He explained that although he didn't know them personally, he did know a bit about brown rats in general and gave them the same lecture as before about all of them, himself included, being indirectly related.

"What have you got against the black rats anyway?" he repeated his earlier question to the brown rats, reversing it as necessary.

"They're filthy" replied one "Carry the plague innit."

"Yeah. It wasn't called the Black Death for nothing" chimed in another.

"For goodness sake!" sighed Maurice "That was over a hundred years ago! You've got to stop living in the past or you'll never be able to move forward."

He told them of the trials and tribulations that he had come up against since being abandoned in the park a couple of days ago and went on to share the details of the discussions that he'd had with their arch-enemies, further down the alley, embellishing his defense of their whole species, particularly the part concerning poor hygiene and the general character assassinations, to suit his present purpose. It seemed to do the trick, as their confrontational stance slowly melted away.

"It's a pleasure to meet you, Mister Maurice" said the main rat "I'm Naz, and these two reprobates are Khan and Ali."

Maurice smiled inwardly to himself, marvelling at the quite distinct comparisons that he was easily able to draw between the two groups; Naz was clearly the leader and Clay's equivalent; Khan scowled at him with exactly the same air of overt hostility that Vander had offered him upon their first meeting, whilst Ali was much more genteel, offering a soft, limp-wristed paw for Maurice to shake. If Maurice was a betting mouse, he would've guessed that there was probably a fairly good chance that he had a sweet tooth too.

"Charmed" said Ali, whilst Khan said nothing, eyeing him suspiciously, forepaws remaining firmly folded across his barrell chest.

"So I can go then?" Maurice ventured.

"Well" said Naz, after a fashion "We can't have you going off into the world and telling everyone that the black rats treated you well but the brown rats didn't, can we? That just wouldn't do our impeccable reputation any good at all, now would it?" He smiled a broad smile which told Maurice that perhaps he had really listened to some of what the little mouse had been trying to tell them after all. Khan complained that their reputation would be ruined anyway if they let Maurice go, that they would be seen as weak, but his insistence was only half hearted, as if he knew that it was expected of him to be contrary and that changing now would have been perceived as losing face and made him look soft too. Naz's answer came without any words even being necessary. He gently pushed his two sidekicks back, positioning them to one side, before stepping backwards himself and waving Maurice on through the gap forged between them. As he stepped through the parted bodies, Maurice hesitated, wishing that he could find some way of letting them see the glaring similarities between themselves and the black rats, how they had fallen into playing stereotypical roles in a tragedy which could easily have had a different script, but he didn't want to push his luck and risk offending them when they were being so amicable towards him.

He didn't look back. He still had to keep reminding himself that he might now be out of the real woods but the metaphorical ones still surrounded him at every turn and were thick with thorny brambles.

Brown Hawk Down

Leaving the heart of the city behind him, Maurice headed for the long, seemingly never-ending stretch of dual carriageway which would hopefully lead him ever nearer to home. This next leg of the journey seemed even more arduous for its lack of significant landmarks or variation in the surrounding landscape; in much the same way that when you're looking out of the porthole window of an aeroplane travelling at five hundred miles per hour, you feel like you're hardly moving. He had nothing ahead of him to gauge how much headway he was making, other than yet more motorway. Each footstep he took seemed to kick the horizon further away so that it appeared never to get any closer. It was as if he was walking the wrong way down an airport passenger treadmill. The landscape to his left and right consisted of gloomily lit woodland, no doubt filled with all manner of lurking unknown dangers which might leap out upon him at any moment, dragging him off kicking and squeaking into the tangled undergrowth; so Maurice kept to the grass verge at the edge of the hard shoulder, hoping also that this would prevent him from getting lost and going round and round in circles. He knew that the house which his family had settled in was by the coast and knew too, from his earlier aerial view at the elevated outcrop on the edge of the woods, that this road ran along close and parallel to the seafront. He wasn't sure if he was heading in the right direction along it, however, as he had no idea how far North or South he'd been dropped off in the first place and he was still yet to see a single one of the large blue road-signs that he'd been so eagerly watching out for. At least it was only a fifty-fifty gamble. These were far better odds than he, or anyone else, would ever have given himself at the beginning of his journey. He just had to hope that his good fortune would hold out a little longer.

Giant articulated lorries rumbled past him in a relentless convoy like migrating dinosaurs, sucking up tiny specks of grit in their unaerodynamic wake, which swirled around in the wind, causing Maurice to squint constantly. He was even forced to stop occassionally when a piece of tiny shrapnel managed to find its way into his eyes, until his rapid blinking and rubbing created the tears required to flush it out again, only to be replaced a few minutes later by another. The open tarmac was also much more exposed than the built-up town and the high banks of trees on either side funnelled the otherwise fairly mild breeze into a stiff, biting wind which made each step forward feel like he was wading through treacle, bombarding his eyes still further with irritating pollen, small storm flies and yet more grit. It didn't help either that it had been a long time now since Maurice had last eaten anything substantial and he was feeling incredibly weary anyway. He counted his blessings that he'd been given such a hearty feed at Brody's. It was hard to believe that, less than forty-eight hours ago, he'd been so uncomfortably full-up with food that he'd thought his little scoff- stretched stomach might burst.

The rustling of the wind stirring through the trees, on either side, played tricks on his overactive imagination, conjuring up thoughts of carnivorous, mouse-eating monsters; and the sweeping beams of light from car headlights rushing past, fell on waxy, dew-glistened leaves, transforming them in his mind into countless pairs of nocturnal eyes, stalking him from the darkness. So resolute was he in his determination to remain extra-vigilant, that Maurice's heightened sensitivity created enhancements and fabrications which actually took the opposite effect and clouded his judgement. He had naively failed to heed Brody's earlier warnings about the trees being filled with owls and hawks. In fact, so intent was he on checking his clear path, that he failed to look up even once, oblivious to the only real clear and present danger, hovering into a headwind high above him.

He remained blissfully unaware that his flagging little figure had become a prime target, fixed firmly in the sniper-sharp sights of the flying ace hovering in the sky, out on a dawn raid, silently monitoring his slow but steady progress below.

The tired little traveller passed orange and white road cones which had closed off the left-hand lane for a distance, for no apparent reason that Maurice could make out. There certainly didn't seem to be any sign of any road-works taking place. He decided to count a hundred bollards before stopping to take a rest and catch his breath. At about cone eighty-four, the kestrel suddenly tucked its wings in close to its side and plummeted downwards towards the unsuspecting mouse at break-neck speed, in a rapid stoop, as if fired from a crossbow. Maurice's guardian angel must still have been looking down on him. At the exact same instant, by a one-in-a-million chance, what can only be described as a miracle happened. A speeding Jaguar saloon in the outside lane set off a speed camera which flashed its strobe-like double flash, taking a freeze-frame of the bird of prey, dazzling her powerful, binocular vision just enough to stall her deadly divebomb and lighting up the surrounding area like a bolt of sheet lightening, creating a giant bird shaped shadow on the ground ahead of Maurice, alerting him to the hunter's incoming attack. The driver of the automobile would never know how close he had come to receiving a speeding ticket through the post, as his vehicle's rear number plate was completely obscured from view by the incidental wildlife footage. Maurice ran for cover, aiming for cone eighty-five, figuring that he could hide behind it from this, as yet unidentified, new threat. He was still extremely vulnerable. The grass verge offered very little cover and his only two other alternatives were the wild wood or a busy three lane carriageway. Neither presented him with a very attractive option. He wondered fleetingly if, nearby, there might be another of the numerous invisible road force-fields that he'd seen so many more of in the town. 'They might stop attacks from the air too', he thought, before realising that he wouldn't have been able to reach the initiator switches anyway; there were unlikely to be any conveniently abandoned bicycle-wheel ladders tethered way out here in the middle of nowhere. Not that there were even any force-fields in sight. This was the longest road that he'd ever followed and, so far, he hadn't come across a single one along its whole length. The hawk's vision cleared and, with a few skilfull wing adjustments, she managed to bring her stalling downward spiral back under control, narrowly avoiding a crash-landing, before regaining altitude, swooping back up into the air to find a new thermal on which to sit and refocus her aim. Meanwhile, Maurice made it to the bollard, skidding to a sliding stop and ducking gingerly behind it. He peered from around the curved edge, looking up into the drab, early morning sky, seeing his silent foe in all her glory for the first time. The magnificent raptor's apparently effortless suspension in the air belied the enormous physical exertion actually required to keep it there, and despite his wish that the bird was anywhere other than here right now, he couldn't help but be impressed by her beautiful lines and how gracefully she moved. The contrast with Rory's earlier crude efforts couldn't have been more stark. Her petite, steel-blue head remained completely motionless atop a chestnut plumage and brindled, creamy undercarriage, as if not connected with the rest of her body; her fearsomely hooked, flesh-tearing beak providing a useful rifle-sight, trained unwaveringly on the little mouse attempting to hide below. Her wings angled downwards at the ends, drawing almost level with the middle of her darker, elegantly fanned tail, drawing a capital letter 'M' against the dusky background. Maurice had a horrible sinking feeling that McMouse Burger was on this morning's menu. He looked frantically around, trying to think on his feet again and come up with yet another solution to this latest life-threatening situation now facing him. The answer lay directly behind him. Looking across to bollard eighty-six, he saw that it was standing on a loose stone at one corner and so, as a result, was not sitting completely flush with the tarmac. This had created a small gap and, from where he stood, it looked to Maurice to be about the same size as the one that he'd slid underneath at the base of the vicarage door when he'd been fleeing from the scene of his house-mouse-breaking and entering and the wrath of the resident church cat. He didn't really have any choice. Before he had a chance to think about all the possible flaws in the plan, he found himself charging across the expanse of open ground towards it. This triggered an immediate, instinctive response from the falcon, which again folded itself into missile position, before dropping from the sky like a stone, launched mouse-ward.

A bird of prey in a stoop is the fastest moving creature on earth and this kestrel was no exception. Maurice could never have hoped to reach the next bollard more quickly than his record-breaking rival. Less than halfway across and she was almost upon him. He didn't stand a chance. He'd never make it. Only a few feet and half a second more and that would be the end of him. All over. He scrunched his little grit-filled eyes tightly closed, in preparation for the inevitable searing pain as the wind-hover's razor-sharp yellow talons sank into his tender little body, plucking him from the ground like a stuffed toy at a fun fair. But it didn't happen. Just at the anticipated moment of certain impact, Maurice was aware of a dark, feline shape suddenly in his peripheral vision, followed by a shrill squawking and the sounds of a collision of bodies immediately behind him. He didn't dare take the time to look back over his shoulder and instead covered the last few yards dash to the plastic cone, slipping under the gap in a sideways roll, hastily dragging his tail in after him like some Incy-ana Jones, Rodent of the Lost Ark, grabbing, at the last possible second, for his nearly abandoned whip. The pleading, fluffy, open-mouthed little kestrel chicks, waiting expectantly back at the nest, would have to go hungry just a little longer today.

Outside the refuge of his conical air-raid shelter, Maurice could make out the sounds of a frantic scuffle, highlighted with agitated shrill chirrips, squawks, squeaks and growls. He lay flat to the ground, trying to get a better look at what was going on out there but was too far away from all the action to see anything, save for a handful of tawny feathers, floating down to the ground near to his face, one landing gently on his nose causing him to sneeze, others swirled around by the wind, as if in the aftermath of some boarding school pillow-fight. Not wishing to push his luck and sitting away from the edge, out of reach of all the kerfuffle going on outside, Maurice kept his eyes fixed upwards, looking at the circle of sky through the cyclindrical hole at the top of his plastic traffic tee-pee, in anticipation of another view of the ornithological fighter pilot, either flying away in retreat, mission aborted, or coming back for a third attempt at breakfast and perhaps her second victim of the morning. He thought by now, after all he'd been through, that nothing could shock him, but what eventually appeared instead, surprised even him.

Reunited

Maurice recoiled with a gasp, unable to believe his eyes at the portrait filling the circular hole, framed just exactly like the lion at the start of an MGM film. Maurice half expected him to roar in just the same deep, guttural way. He wasn't yet sure if this latest development offered even more of a threat than his previous, airborne, assailant had. Instead though, fixing him a broad, wide-eyed grin, chin all matted pink with a mixture of blood, saliva and a few creamy, downy neck feathers, his rescuer announced his arrival, quickly putting paid, once and for all, to Maurice's initial apprehensions.

"Mornin' boy" came the cheerful greeting.

"Magwitch!" exclaimed a still rather shell-shocked Maurice.

"The very same. Ever at your service my boy. As promised."

"You managed to get free then?" Maurice stated the obvious. He was genuinely glad.

"All thanks to you my boy. All thanks to you. One good turn deserves another I reckon, but a turn like what you done me deserves a hundred back and then some more on top. Risked your life for me you did and I ain't never gonna forget it."

"Anyone would've done the same" said Maurice, modestly, hoping that Magwitch wouldn't believe him.

"Not true" retorted Magwitch "Not true at all. Can't say I blame you for not hangin' around at the end there neither. Good survival instincts you showed, my boy, and nothin' more nor less. You could've just left me there in the first place though but you didn't. Most would've. But not my boy 'ere. You're a true gentlemouse an' no mistakin'."

"It was nothing, really" Maurice continued to downplay his heroic rescue, mildly embarrassed but relishing the adulation in equal measures all at the same time.

"Nothing?" contested Magwitch. "Nothing! Saved my life you did! No-one ever done nothing like that for me before. I owe you a debt of gratitude my boy and I always intend to make it a business of mine to repay my debts. If you're ever in a tight spot again or need a favour, no matter how large or small, I'll never be far away. Just say the word!"

Maurice stroked his whiskers, ruefully, considering Magwitch's generous offer, not wishing to look a gift horse in the mouth and pass up such a golden, once in a lifetime opportunity as this. A mischevous grin crossed his face.

"Actually" he replied "There *is* something that you can do."

Return to Rat Alley

The return journey was considerably easier than it had been coming the other way. The gentle but energy sapping incline, which had caused Maurice's tiny calf muscles to ache so on the way out of town, was reversed and the earlier headwind was now buffeting at his behind, nudging him gently along downhill at a much more agreeable pace. With Magwitch by his side, he didn't have to worry so much about attacks from predators either and so progress was made with much longer, more confident strides, compared with his previous, fear-restricted little pigeon steps. He effectively had his own personal bodyguard now and it felt great. A small part of him even half-hoped that some prowling, unsuspecting creature *would* leap out at him from the bushes, only to be sent packing, tail between their legs, when they saw the carnivorous company that he was now keeping. He knew that they wouldn't dare though. In fact, Maurice was quite certain that even another mink would probably think twice before daring to tackle the terrible Magwitch.

What an unlikely pairing the two of them made. If only The Major could see him now, thought Maurice, strutting fearlessly along next to such a blood-thirsty savage. He'd give anything to see the look of awe and admiration on his father's face.

Coming back into the town centre was significantly less hazardous than his first visit had been. It was by now the early hours of day-break and all was perfectly still and grey and calm. The streets were empty of people, save for a single postman, riding along on his creaking, black, old-fashioned push-bike, tunelessly whistling a merry tune. All the bustling bars and clubs of the night before had long since closed to the last of the stumbling stragglers and the only transport that they came across was a battery-powered milk float which whirred past, the milkman at the wheel still not yet sufficiently fully awake to notice the two of them as he slowly overtook, glass bottles chinking gently in their plastic crates behind him. Maurice's delicate, velvety ears twitched as he became vaguely aware, from within a number of the properties that they passed, of the occasional muffled electronic beeping of bedside alarm-clock radios, announcing 'time to get up' to the snoring figures slumbering peacefully next to them, pressing the snooze buttons one too many times as usual.

Eventually they turned the corner which would lead them on to the high street. Maurice gave a few last minute instructions to his mustelid minder, before parting company to go off a short way ahead of him. He almost didn't recognise the alleyway until he was directly upon it. The neon dancing girls were now dull, unilluminated grey tubes, barely noticeable in the rapidly growing daylight, and an abandoned supermarket trolley had been left, carelessly parked across its entrance – presumably used to transport a drunken reveller at least part of the way home last night.

Apart from these temporary, superficial differences, however, not much else had changed. Despite all of his very best intentions, Maurice had still not yet succeeded in permanently altering the ratty residents' way of thinking. The two groups had continued to remain separate; the black rats sitting around on their steps, insulting their rivals and hatching dastardly plots to take overall control of the territory, with the brown rats doing much the same in return, at the other end. Maurice felt certain that his words had definitely made some impact at the time, however fleeting, but things had gotten back to the normal old routine all too quickly. He knew that, to such an uneducated, motley crew as this, action would surely speak louder than words if he were to have any hope of making a lasting difference.

Maurice took a deep breath, filling his lungs with as much of the crisp morning air as he could, to prepare for the next phase of his plan. 'Okay' he muttered to himself 'You want to play your silly games? Well say hello to my little friend!' and launched into a sprint, running as fast as his little legs would carry him; which, to be fair, wasn't really very fast at all. He sped along the length of the alleyway, waiting until he'd nearly drawn level with the steps where the black rats dozed, among the discarded debris, before shouting at the top of his voice "Help! Help! Somebody save me! Save yourselves!"

The bleary-eyed rats stirred, wearily raising their sleep-heavy heads to see what all the fuss was about.

"Eh?" they mumbled, still not quite with it and more than a little surprised to see little Maurice charging past, back with them again so soon after the rare reprieve that they'd granted him.

"Behind you!" he warned back to them, pointing up the path as he ran. As their heads turned slowly in that direction, the rabid figure of Magwitch in hot pursuit careered into view, silhouetted against the light from the pavement outside the alley, strings of drool flying from his snarling muzzle.

"Ferret!" screamed Vander, in a high pitched squeal that betrayed his earlier tough-rat persona. Maurice gleefully savoured the reaction. Revenge was sweet. As sweet as Battenberg itself.

"I'm not a stinkin' ferret! I'm a bloomin' mink" complained an exasperated Magwitch, in between his exaggerated pretence of aggressive spitting and hissing. He ran with just enough speed to look like he meant business, without ever allowing himself to gain on Maurice or catch up with the rats too soon. This was just as well for them at this particular instance because being incorrectly identified was fast becoming a serious pet-hate of his. In the heat of the moment, he might not have stuck rigidly to the original plan. He was starting to develop something of an identity crisis, almost a match for Angus's, if the truth be known.

The brown rats, meanwhile, had been woken by all the commotion further down the alley and shuffled down from their step, scratching the backs of their heads, stretching, arcing their spines and rubbing their eyelids just in time to see the tiny mouse dash urgently past, calling for them to 'Run for your lives!'

A glance down the alley revealed the alarming stampede of approaching black rats, bounding, panic-stricken, towards them, the ferocious, furry, fanged fiend hot on their gristly tails. Armoured cockroaches scuttled and scattered in every direction, out of harm's way, lining up at the edge of the walls to enjoy the early morning carnival and revelling in the opportunity to see the rats fleeing for *their* lives for a change. It was nice to see them getting a taste of their own medicine. Usually it was them doing the chasing. Now the shoe was on the other foot. Or not, as the case may be.

"Cat!" screamed Khan as, once again, the supposed heavy of the gang was the first to show his terror.

Magwitch just rolled his eyes in despair "I'm not a cat. I'm a ......oh, what's the point!?" he muttered, realising that it was a waste of time, and carrying on regardless.

All was going precisely as planned and Maurice was having a whale of a time. He'd gained quite a lead on the rest of the animals, allowing him time to pull up to an abrupt, skidding halt by the corner of one of the coal bunkers that he'd remembered passing last night. He'd noticed then that the door had been left unbolted and ever so slightly ajar. He'd been quite clear on this fact because he'd had to wash his feet in a clean puddle later on where the coal-dust had turned the puddles on the alley floor into ink, making it look like he was wearing black ankle socks and leaving a trail of dark paw-prints following after him, betraying his location to any would-be animal assassin. He remembered thinking that, until then, he hadn't fully understood exactly what was meant by this 'carbon footprint' that everyone seemed to be so concerned about lately. He was relieved to see that the door was still exactly as he'd last seen it and hadn't since been re-fastened shut. He had to work quickly. With every ounce of available strength left at his disposal, Maurice pulled at the corner of the door where he calculated that he'd get the most leverage. It had been a long time since the rusty hinges had last seen any grease and the movement was stiff, making the task feel like the Corgi Truck-Pull at a strong-mouse contest. It's amazing what the body is capable of when pumped full of adrenaline and desperate determination though. Maurice's eyes bulged and his cheeks coloured purple as, with a final almighty heave, the sound of creaking metal could be heard and ferrous orange flakes fell to the ground, indicating a slow but definite yielding as he managed to create a distinct gap; a gap just big enough for a fleeing rat to fit through.

The black rats, having had a head-start, were the first to reach the point where Maurice stood, leaning coolly on the edge of the coal bunker door.

"Quickly! In here!" he called, in a shouted whisper - if such a thing exists.

The black rats filed in without hesitation, grateful for somewhere dark to hide.

"Get right to the back, where you can't be seen" instructed Maurice, keen to make sure that they went right in, and they did as they were told, only too glad of someone to take charge and make an executive decision amidst such pandemonium.

Having a potentially ravenous mink chomping at your heels makes you run pretty fast when you're a rodent and the brown rats weren't far behind, arriving at the same point just as the last of the black rats had slipped completely out of sight.

"Over here" called Maurice again, gesturing to the narrow opening between the door and its frame. "Get inside, quickly!" and again, they followed his orders without question.

As the last inch of thick rubbery pink tail disappeared from view, Maurice leant both his forepaws against the rotted wooden door and, with them locked out straight in front of him, proceeded to attempt to push it back again, as hard as he could. His feet slipped and slid, failing to get a good grip on the grimy pavement this time, and he worried that he wouldn't get it closed as he'd hoped, until a helpful last minute shoulder shove from Magwitch saw the door slam to with a resounding thud.

The pair of them banged loudly against the door, deliberately sending waves of blind panic through the temporary inhabitants inside, who ran around in the darkness tripping over each other and coughing and spluttering through the thick clouds of dust that they were whipping up. The two of them kept this up until Maurice was happy that the rats had been moving around in there long enough for his thus far perfectly executed plan to take effect. He silently gave Magwitch the thumbs up to signal that he should go and wait at the rendez-vous point, as agreed, and Magwitch loped off, out of the alley and just around the corner. When he was happy that his accomplice could no longer be seen, Maurice called to the rats inside. "Hey, it's just me! Maurice! It's ok, he's gone, you can come out now!"

"H-h-how do we know it's safe?" came the nervous, unconvinced reply from within.

"Would I still be out here, talking to you now, if it wasn't?" answered Maurice. He'd already anticipated just such a question when hatching the plan in the first place so had his answer ready immediately; although he effected the briefest of pauses, barely discernible but just long enough to seem genuine and so disguise his premeditation. It was a good point.

"I guess not / I suppose / He's right / That's true" came the assorted responses from the other side.

"Now all of you need to push against the door" called Maurice "I don't have the strength left to open it again on my own and my feet are all slippery now."

There was a sound of stumbling around from within. Lumps of coal rolled down, hitting against the inside of the wooden door, as they were disturbed by the rats jostling for position and then the door swung slowly open once again. The rats all emerged together, cautiously at first, warily peering up and down the length of the alleyway for any sign of a follow-up ambush. When none came they seemed to react as one, breathing a collective sigh of relief. The surge of adrenalin, mixed with their elation at surviving near slaughter, caused them to whoop and holler their celebration at still being alive. They shook paws, gave each other high-fours and hugged the rat nearest to them, jumping up and down with their fore-paws around one another and singing songs of a bravery that, in reality, they hadn't really shown. Every single one of them was covered from head to toe in thick soot, their fur completely dulled of any shine, so that they looked almost like matt, three-dimensional shadows of their former selves.

"Hey, look at us" laughed Khan, to the rat that he was dancing with "We look just like black rats!" and with that Ali looked at his dance partner too and Naz at the rat that he was embracing and they all chuckled their agreement.

Maurice stood at the edge of the party and spoke in a firm but even tone, without raising his voice at all. "That's because they are"

"What are you talking about" growled Khan

"Your dance partner" observed Maurice "*Is* a black rat. Look at his ear!"

Khan stared in disbelief at the figure opposite him. It was Vander. He knew that torn lobe anywhere. He should do. He'd done it himself.

"But I thought..." mumbled Vander, incredulously.

"You thought *what* exactly?" probed Maurice

"I thought they were black rats too"

"Well we thought you were brown rats" explained Naz, getting involved "Just dirty ones"

"Well, the only thing that's changed is that you're now all the same colour. For the moment at least" Maurice pointed out to them. "Now if that's all it takes to make you think you're all the same, then are you really all that different underneath?"

A long silent pause followed, pregnant perhaps with a few years worth of regrets.

Clay looked across at Naz. "That was pretty close huh?"

"A little too close for comfort" agreed his counterpart.

"Did you see the size of his teeth?" marvelled Ali.

"They needed a good clean" added Sugar-Ray, from his metaphorical glass house "They were pink."

"I could feel his breath on my back, he was so close" came another voice.

"Lucky for him he caught us by surprise innit?" Khan puffed out his chest.

"Yeah. Too right" supported Vander "One of him against six of us. It would have been no contest" - and he was probably right, although not in the way that he meant, of course.

"Seven" mused Clay.

"Seven?" came the quizzical chorus of replies from the rest of the group.

"You said one of him against six of us. You forgot little Maurice. That makes seven. If it wasn't for him....."

"Hey, where is he?" they all looked around, but the little grey mouse was nowhere to be seen. "He really helped us."

"He certainly did" agreed Clay, still wondering how come little Maurice had inexplicably managed to stay on the other side of the coal-bunker door and live to tell the tale, apparently completely unharmed. He looked down from the step where he stood at the five grubby figures looking up at him and then to the ground, at the two mismatched sets of dark footprints, one distinctly larger than the other, leading out of the alleyway, side by side. "I have a feeling he helped us more than we'll ever know."

Meanwhile, back out of town once again, Maurice and Magwitch had reached the point where they'd met for the second time, midway between traffic cones eighty-five and eighty-six. Following a brief spell of self congratulatory celebration, with laughter, chests bumped against chests, leaping hugs and a final high four for good measure, the mood suddenly became more sober.

"Well boy. This is me. Until the next time."

"Where will you go?" asked Maurice, saddened by the prospect of travelling alone and vulnerable again but knowing that it was unavoidable.

"Ask me no questions an' I'll tell ya no lies boy" Magwitch winked at him. "But I just wanna say one thing, before we parts company. T'was a noble thing what you just done there. Goin' all that way back when you're all small like you are an' you'd come so far an' all. You didn't owe them hoods nothin'. You didn't 'ave to do it but you went on right ahead an' done it nonetheless."

"You did it too" Maurice reminded him, modestly deflecting some of the praise.

"Aah yes, but t'was your idea boy. And a mighty fine one it was at that if I may be so bold as to say so. I've learnt a thing or two from you these past few days my boy. A good few lessons. You should be a teacher when you gets older an' no mistakin'."

A teacher! Maurice like the sound of that. That way he could get to stay at his precious school forever.

"And you could be a careers adviser" suggested Maurice, in a tone somewhere halfway between sincere and something else.

"No boy, the straight an' narrer aint fer me I'm afraid. I aint cut out to be no desk-jockey. A career criminal, maybe"

"Well, so long Magwitch. Thanks for all your help"

"So long boy" replied the mink, already wandering off up a slope, heading into the woods, no doubt with some new mischief already on his mind . As Maurice started to count another hundred cones to help pass the time, Magwitch called after him, one last time, before he'd even managed to get into double figures.

"Hey Maurice!"

"Yes?"

"Just one more thing boy!"

"Yes?"

"I never really had an associate watching you when I was stuck there in that trap. Yer 'eart and lungs are perfectly safe. I'm sorry I lied. I made it up cos I was desperate. I did what I 'ad to do."

Maurice smiled at him. "I know" he said, imitating the wink that he'd just learned from Magwitch - and the mink's return smile spread even broader, filled with even more affection for the plucky little fellow than it was already.

End of the Rocky Road

The unmistakable taste and smell of marsh mud and cast-off seaweed in his nostrils was enough to confirm to a delighted Maurice that he had finally and, quite unbelievably, made it back to the coast. He scampered along the steadily busying promenade, which was coming back to life as the rest of the world slowly awoke for another day, taking in the delights of the day-tripper haven. Early rising locals crunched along the shingle and sea-smoothed pebbles, heads down earnestly seeking lengths of beached driftwood to throw, for their excited, tail-wagging, tongue-lolling dogs to chase after and retrieve. A bedraggled Jack Russell terrier, returning from a rather chilly, over-zealous dip, shook itself damp in a spray of salt-water, to the reluctant, mixed amusement of its sodden owner. A pair of middle-aged women, clothed from head-to-toe in the latest, expensive designer sportswear, jogged past at barely more than their usual walking pace, listening to motivational high-energy dance music on their personal stereos. Maurice wondered why they bothered arranging to run with a friend, only to then completely ignore each other. Lycra-clad, cyclists cruised silently past, hunched over the handlebars, legs pumping like rhythmic pistons, the riders keeping their be-helmeted heads down as low as possible in an effort to gain any slight advantage that they could, reduce drag and avoid a face-full of flying insects. A blonde-ponytailed, somewhat unseasonally bronzed roller-skater, dressed more appropriately for mid-summer weather in her lime-green cropped vest and hot-pants, scissored and swerved along backwards, slaloming through the few pedestrians savouring the bracing sea air. A very smartly presented, elderly gentleman, sporting immaculately pressed, battleship blue-grey, flannel trousers with creases like razors, half strolled, half marched back from the corner shop, a perfectly folded newspaper tucked neatly under his arm, like a rifleman on parade. Most of these were familiar sights to Maurice, but he had never fully appreciated them that much before. They had been of merely a little interest; part of the background scenery which he'd never really paid too much attention to. Everything that he looked at now filled him with a feeling of security and jubilation; and nothing more so than the sight of the Victorian pleasure pier, jutting out into the mud, to at least half a mile from the shore, reaching wistfully after the recently departed tide. He realised with crystal clarity that, for the first time, he knew exactly where he was. Nearly home.

Endowed with a renewed vigour, fuelled with a second (or third or fourth or perhaps even fifth?) wind, he followed the cycle lane, moving at an energetic pace, remaining, for the most part, unseen, underneath the cars parked kerbside, all the way along the whole length of the road. He must have unknowingly passed directly beneath at least half a dozen cats, relaxing in blissfull ignorance atop the warm, recently driven, bonnets above, paws tucked in beneath them; like novelty tea-cosies. To his right, plump herring-gulls braved the coastal elements, balance-beamed on the mossy, algae-covered wave-breakers. Those that didn't, circled directly above, calling vociferously to their companions to come and join them on the wing. From the impressive size of them, thought Maurice, the waters round here clearly offered some pretty healthy pickings. In fact, so plump were they, that he was amazed that they could even get off of the ground.

As Maurice's walking pace turned into an eager jog, he was about to find out that he had indeed been missed after all. More so, in fact, than he could ever have imagined. What he'd remained completely oblivious to, right up until now, was that in his absence he had inadvertently become something of a local legend. Word of his adventures had spread like wild-fire through the bush-telegraph and found its way back to his otherwise quite uneventful suburban home neighbourhood, chiefly via the much more mobile, larger range-spanning sparrows and starlings. This previously anonymous little figure was now attracting fascinated attention as he was recognised by the numerous animal residents of the area and the rumours of his return circulated rapidly around the rest of the local community. Other mice came out of their homes to get a good look at their new champion, the younger ones stopping play to join in and run along behind him. Lizards, only just about thawed out from the previous cold night air, in the first of the morning sun's rays, joined in too, their stiffened joints at first creaking but soon loosening up as they went until they reached their full, unorthodox, panic-style gait, somewhat akin to that of a child trying to escape being chased and tickled. A lithe, athletic-looking frog leapt (leap-frogged, I guess you could say) after him, hopping over the warty, rather more portly lumbering figure of a following natterjack toad, as if to confound the similarities between them. Overhead, swifts and swallows darted and divebombed expertly here and there, like a smokeless red arrow dsiplay team. A robin gave up on his morning tug-of-war, allowing the struggling worm a lucky escape. This particular early bird was happy to give up his advantage today to join in the chase, along with, by now, a wren, two house sparrows, three starlings, two blackbirds (a male and female couple), one thrush, a selection of assorted-coloured finches (two chaffinches, one bullfinch, one goldfinch and a greenfinch), three beetles, eight mice (three adults and five young), four earwigs, four pigeons (one with only one complete leg – a number of others remained, screw-top heads swivelling, jostling for position atop their favourite lamp-posts because the view was good from up there), an orderly procession of soldier ants, marching in formation and, lagging behind somewhat, bringing up the rear (by quite a long way back in fact) and leaving a silvery trail for latecomers to follow - a snail named Carl.

The steadily forming parade boosted Maurice's vim still further until he almost thought that he could hear an imaginary brass band playing in his head. His jog became gradually faster and faster, until he turned the last corner, into the road at the back of Tom's flat, breaking into a near sprint for the final surge to the steps; the rest of the frenzied fun-run still desperately keen to keep up with him at any cost. They wanted to witness his making it all the way home for themselves so that they could one day tell their grand-children that they were there when it happened, when the all-conquering hero returned. They wanted to be a part of natural history in the making.

Arriving at the steps, Maurice was so euphoric that he would have leapt them three or four at a time, were it not for his being so small, but instead had to settle for just clambering up them a little quicker than usual. With the laughing, clapping crowd behind him, cheering him on and chanting 'MAU-RICE! MAU-RICE! MAU-RICE!' this didn't take him long at all; probably less than half the time of his previous personal best in fact, although there is no official time on record. Once at the top of the wooden staircase, standing on the square platform, his gold-medal podium, outside the kitchen door from where it had all begun, Maurice punched the air in exhilaration, shadow-boxing in an adrenalin-fuelled celebration, dancing and leaping from foot to foot, a pugilistic Maurice dance, raising his fore-paws up in the air in victorious pose, feeding on the frenzied hysteria below, at the foot of the steps and saluting his adoring public, milking the moment, loving every minute of it. Sure, he'd been up against the ropes many times but, when most would have expected him to go down in the first round, he'd never thrown in the towel. He had taken on the world and gone the distance. All three miles of it.

Home Sweet Home

As the furore below died down and the crowds began to disperse, Maurice climbed the upright beam which fastened the wooden outer staircase to the rendered outside upstairs kitchen wall until he arrived at the section of tubular grey plastic waste pipe which transported the dirty water, from the washing machine inside, to the drainage system outside. He hoisted himself onto it, straddling it just as he had the can of Orca fizzy drink when he'd paddled across what he now referred to as 'Pike Pond' (it would, much later, become known the whole world over as 'Loch Lucius' and establish itself as part of mouse folklore. Mice would come from far and wide to stare, transfixed, at the gently rippling waters in the hope of spotting the legendary 'Lucy' and unending debate would ensue over the authenticity of any number of ambiguously blurred photographs of the 'monster' which were denounced as hoaxes by experts but fiercely defended as the genuine article by their vehement owners). Shimmying along its length, he took care not to inadvertently glance downward. He wasn't good with heights and it simply wouldn't do to fall now at this final, relatively insignificant hurdle after all the others that he'd overcome against such seemingly insurmountable odds. Eventually he reached the one and a half inch gap in the brick wall, all around the pipe's circumference, where it entered into the first floor flat. Luckily for Maurice, Tom was still yet to realize that this was the point from which his mouse problem had originated and that it remained still, to this day, the sole access point of entry and exit for the rest of Maurice's family; not to mention all manner of other creepy crawlies . As such, it hadn't yet been blocked up as had so often been the case in the past, at previous residences, where Maurice had betrayed their location to the proprietor. To tell the truth, Tom hadn't really considered it to be that much of a problem at all and hadn't worried too much since removing the first and, or so he thought, only mouse. Ever since his catching Maurice, the rest of the mouse family had taken extra special care to remain even more discrete than usual, giving away no sight, sound or sign whatsoever which might have alerted their unwitting host to their presence here, sharing his home without contributing so much as a penny towards the mortgage. Subsequently unconcerned, Tom hadn't carried out any further, follow-up investigation into a possible infestation and so hadn't noticed the gap. Even if he had seen it, it was unlikely that he would ever have believed that anything short of a stick insect could fit through such a tiny space. It is fortunate for them, though, that mice are often underestimated in this way. In actual fact, every member of Maurice's family, even including the comparitively strapping, broad-shouldered Major, could squeeze through quite comfortably, so dinky little Maurice found doing so no problem at all.

Dropping into the sheltered warmth of the indoor kitchenette, Maurice suddenly appreciated how cold it had become outside in the last few days. His fur stood on end over the gooosebumps on his skin beneath and he wasn't sure if it was just from the change in temperature or the mixture of emotions that he was feeling; the euphoria of a few moments earlier outside, near hyserical relief and excitement at making it home to see his family again and nervous apprehension at what sort of welcome he was likely to receive. Would his father be happy to see his youngest son, safely back, or would he be livid at Maurice having broken his promise not to go beyond the imposed boundaries? Perhaps they were all glad to have seen the back of him, pleased that he'd gone missing, never again to blow their cover and provoke another unwelcome eviction. He thought that at least his mum would probably have been upset. Were they even still here? Had they moved on elsewhere, leaving no forwarding address? Had they themselves perhaps been caught and released into the countryside too? Or worse? Were they even still alive? Why, when the whole neighbourhood had come out to greet him, weren't they there too? Maurice felt dizzy with all of these unanswered questions swimming around inside his head. There was nothing else for it. Just as he had done before making his return charge down Rat Alley, he took a long, deep, drawn out breath of resignation and disappeared down the crevice between the kitchen units and the washing machine. He was hopefully about to find out.

.

Family Reunion

As it turned out, Maurice's homecoming was not altogether a complete surprise to his family after all. Word of his imminent arrival had been difficult to avoid. It was all anybody in the area had been talking about for hours and the ever increasing flow of incoming birds, chirping and twittering excitedly of little else had confirmed that it must surely be true, each new voice further eradicating the possibility that such talk might be merely some kind of urban myth. Indeed, if the Major, Mary and the twins hadn't expected him by now, then the uproarious din from outside only moments before had certainly made sure that they did now. Rather than join the others though and be lost as just another insignificant set of faces in the crowd, they'd decided to offer him a more personal ceremony at the most fitting of venues; his long aimed-for target destination – home. As Maurice dropped down through the hole in the floorboards and arrived finally at the entrance to the family domain, he was met immediately with all four of them, waiting expectantly, every bit as nervous as him, maybe even more so, ready to receive their estranged relation.

Maurice stood still in the opening, taking in an image before his eyes that he had, at one point, thought that he might very probably never see again. For once, he was glad to be wrong. They seemed to do the same thing in return, all five of them standing there, motionless, silent, incredulous. This pause allowed Maurice time to fully take in the whole scene and notice what lay to their left, slightly behind them all. An impressive smorgasboard of cakes and sweets had been laid out, a veritable Aladdin's cave of confectionery. This treacly treasure trove contained ruby coloured glace cherries stolen from atop French fancies, golden syrup soaked sponge, pastries encrusted with diamonds of sugar and all manner of other calorific jewels, gathered together by Maurice's family and donated by well-wishing friends and neighbours. The smaller morsels surrounded the dominant centre-piece; a large rectangle of pink and yellow Battenberg, made up of the carefully shaped jigsaw of pieces of other smaller Battenberg cakes, joined together with apricot jam and framed by similarly sourced sections of sticky marzipan. Written in red aniseed liquorice shoelaces atop this cake canvass was the message 'Welcome Home Maurice'.

On reading this, Maurice realised for the first time that his worst fears and reservations had been unfounded. He had been missed. He smiled and this was all the trigger that was needed for his family to respond. His mother was the first to break the silent tension and rushed forward, sweeping her prodigal son up in her arms in a loving hug, squeezing him so tightly and smothering him with so many kisses that he could hardly breathe. Not that he minded one little bit on this occassion. The long deep-breath that he'd taken before turning the final corner of his journey, would just have to last him a little longer, that was all.

"How did you manage to write that?" he asked, referring to the message on the cake, aware of his family's academic limitations.

"Your school had an appeal" blurted Mary, through her joyful sobs, her face muffled in Maurice's neck. "The English class wrote it for us. We've been out searching every night. We never gave up hope. Not for a second."

Next it was the turn of the twins to squeak, surrounding him, trying to get a look in past their mother's formidable, suffocating clutches, desperate for their little brother's attention.

"We've heard so many stories!" exclaimed Barry

"Yeah" chimed in Robin "You're a national hero!" In fact, 'regional' might actually have been more accurate at this stage; 'national' would come a little later, with time.

"We heard you fought an eagle, single-handed" came Barry again

"Made the heavyweight look like a featherweight" finished off Robin, on this particular story at least. And on they went, jabbering feverishly away, tales of epic battles with fearsome foes:

"Wrestled a shark...."

"Trapped a whole army of killer rats......"

"Had them pleading for forgiveness....."

"Out-ran a panther........"

"Tied a boa constrictor in knots....."

"Dove under a juggernaut to save a hedgehog from certain death......"

"Made a stoat your slave........."

"It wasn't a ...... " interjected Maurice half-heartedly, before deciding that perhaps now wasn't really the time to explain.

"Is it all true then?" Barry almost pleaded for Maurice, their new third Mousketeer,   to answer in the affirmative.

"More or less" conceded Maurice, too weary to go into detail and not wishing to disappoint his bravado hungry brothers. Well they were close enough after all. Anything else was just details.

Realising from his general demeanour that maybe they were over-crowding him, the family parted, stepping away to give

Maurice some space, leaving the upright, ever-regimental figure of The Major, standing awkwardly to attention before him. He wasn't a mouse generally given to displays of public affection, or emotion of any kind for that matter.

Maurice looked deep into his eyes, recognising something that he hadn't seen in them before and that he thought he never would. A tear. Just one maybe, but undeniably a tear nonetheless. His eyes were all misty looking and pink; as if he'd been crying a lot before now, over the past few days. Dark circles sat beneath them too. He looked tired; as if he hadn't been sleeping.

"Hi dad" mouthed Maurice, not sure that any sound actually came out.

His father stepped forward, reached as if to shake his son's paw in his own, before thinking better of it and changing his mind, moved in closer instead to lift him up in a crushing, heartfelt embrace; something else that Maurice had never known before. Placing his rough, calloused paws on Maurice's tiny shoulders, he stepped back, holding him out at arm's length to get a good look at him, as if making absolutely certain for one last time that it was really him. Then he spoke for the first time, his voice cracking slightly as he did, so that he had to repeat himself.

"Welcome home son. Welcome home."

And start all over again

A few days later and all the hysteria surrounding little Maurice had settled down. He'd been inundated with visitors, beseiged by every mammal, insect, reptile, amphibian and bird that he'd come across in the past seventy-two hours, all wanting to hear stories of his now legendary adventures out in the big wide world. News of his exploits would later become global, spread first as far as North Africa by the excited, patriotic tweets and chirrups of spine-tailed swifts and swallows journeying South for the winter and, later, across the Atlantic to Canada, on the beaks of migrating geese and Hooper swans.

For the fourth time in less than a week, Maurice had been allowed to lie in and recuperate, remaining asleep until he was ready to wake of his own accord, to help build his strength back up. Only last week, when he'd been left to sleep past 6am, his father had argued with Mary that she was molly-coddling him. This time, it was on the Major's own insistent recommendation that he remain bed-bound. 'His son', as he now constantly referred to Maurice, had earned it. Mary reminded her husband good-naturedly that Maurice was still her son too; but this was competition for her son's affections that she could happily live with.

Having slowly stirred and motivated himself to finally get up, wash and face the world, Maurice cleaned his teeth that morning for even longer than the required five minutes that was his father's usual express wish, fondly remembering Sugar-Ray's enamel-less, magnolia smile. He was hungry. Starving in fact. The buffet of party delicacies collected for him only days before had not lasted very long at all, what with all the guests that they'd entertained since his return, all wishing to hear the incredible stories for themselves. The family had gone out foraging for breakfast but Maurice didn't think that he could necessarily wait long enough for them to get back. He needed to go and find himself something to eat *right now*.

Not wishing to be barraged with requests for autographs or yet another animated account of his trip, Maurice decided not to go outside and instead to make his way up through the floorboards, to see if any morsels might have been accidentally dropped from the kitchen worktop onto the floor above and not yet swept up. All had been quiet for some time. He hadn't heard or felt any walking around overhead and so was confident that the coast should be clear. From the amount of daylight streaming in through the kitchen window, the position of the sun in the sky and the resultant length of the shadows formed by the kitchen table legs, he deduced that it was quite clearly well past the time that Tom usually always left for work in the mornings anyway. What he didn't know though, due mostly to the fact that he'd lost all track of time lately, what with all the fuss and flap surrounding his return and having missed school whilst he recuperated, was that today was Saturday.

Having made his way to the edge of the curfew zone without having seen anything remotely edible, Maurice weighed up his options. He could either return home and wait for his family to come back with their booty, which might not even be very much, if anything at all, or he could venture out, just a little further, into the living room area. Tom often ate his meals from a plate on his lap, in front of the television. There were bound to be all sorts of crumbs of who knew what tantalising treats, on the floor nearby or down the sides of the cushions. He'd travelled the world for goodness sake, or some of it at least. He was the most celebrated nomad in mouse history. What possible harm could a few extra feet into the lounge make?

He scampered to the area where he'd last been rumbled, whilst rustling through the refuse bags of food waste. When he got there again, this time, rather than discovering a crumpled black plastic sack, he found himself looking at his own elongated reflection, as if in a fun-fair house of mirrors. Where the wantonly discarded bags had once lain, there now stood a brand-new, shiny, chrome-plated pedal-bin. The sticky label with the sale price on hadn't even been removed yet. He seemed somehow bigger than he had before the whole episode of capture, release and return and it wasn't necessarily due solely to the distorted image. He continued on to the corner of the breakfast bar, looking around the base of the two swivel stools there; often a likely hunting ground for tasty tit-bits, but still without any luck. Tom had obviously become a little more house-proud since discovering that he had a guest, as had so often been the case at other houses where Maurice had given the game away for his family in the past. Food, once recklessly left out, uncovered for vital hours was now stored safely away, sealed in inaccessible, vacuum-packed tupperware containers. In fact, this had been the cause of many family arguments and contributed to the Major's disappointment in his youngest son's inability to develop any sort of independence or survival instincts of his own. He had even tried to use it as a way of persuading Mary that Maurice should join Mouse Cadets but she had remained vehement in her defense of their childrens' right to make their own choices and follow their own paths in life. And that's what Maurice intended to do right now; follow his own path, on to the front room and the comfy three-seater sofa.

Rounding the final corner of the wooden room divide, he surveyed the scene, assessing the safest, least exposed route. A large book-case covered virtually the whole of the far wall, off to his left, filled with CD's, DVD's (among them, 'Stuart Little', although the significance of this was, of course, lost on Maurice), a collection of prized old vinyl records, numerous chunky, well-thumbed reference books, picture frames with assorted images of Tom, his friends and family and a few die-cast model cars, parked up there for the foreseeable future. If only they'd been real, he could have done with one of those a few days ago, thought Maurice, eyeing a nice shiny one eighteenth scale replica of a convertible Ferrari; just the right size for a wannabe Stirling Mouse. A dust-covered, apparently hardly ever used electric guitar stood quietly on a display stand in one corner, clearly more ornamental than instrumental, and a large, widescreen TV took pride of place in the centre of the room, facing directly opposite the settee, quite clearly intended as the main focus of attention. Maurice traversed the thick, tangled sheep-skin rug, to the foot of the sofa, confident of finding something worth nibbling on. But still nothing. The upright green and purple vacuum cleaner stood proudly by the entrance to the sitting room, just out in the hallway, still plugged in at the wall, Maurice noticed through the glass panelled internal door. It was obviously getting a lot more use now than it used to, if the volume of dust and fluff on show in the cylindrical plastic display case was anything to go by. Tom had clearly taken his housework duties to previously unknown levels of fanatical thoroughness. Maurice still wasn't too disheartened though. People were often fussy about their carpets and flooring, he pondered, but they rarely took the same level of care when it came to their furniture. Only on the occassional full annual spring clean did any of the previous residents that they had shared with remove the cushions and hoover the chairs and seating areas underneath as well. Down the backs of most peoples' sofas was usually an 'all you can eat' lucky-dip bouncy buffet of culinary delights.

Maurice climbed the front of the sofa, his tiny hooked claws easily securing a good grip on the textured fabric. He scaled it in no time, with minimal effort, certainly more adeptly than his previous efforts at following Jethro up to his nest; the increased upper-body strength that he had developed over the past few weeks surely helping. Finally, sitting triumphantly atop the plumped-up cushion, he was able to appreciate the vantage point which was Tom's own on most weekday evenings, after he had gotten home from work. With a little rummaging around, he managed to find a few stale toast crumbs, a dried-out mouldy chip, one of Pam's long-lost ear-rings and thirty-seven pence in loose change; but still no sign of anything sufficiently substantial to even wet his by now voracious appetite.

As he struggled up from a gap in the cushions, reaching around for a claw-hold to pull himself up and out, Maurice accidentally placed his fumbling paw against the 'ON' button on the remote-control device left lieing there. The TV screen burst instantly into life and, as a panic-stricken Maurice fumbled around in an effort to turn it off again, he instead pressed the volume button, turning the sound up to an ear-splitting level; certainly loud enough for a dozing Tom to hear from his bedrooom, further down the hallway, and loud enough to block out the sound of his approaching footsteps as he got up to see what on earth was going on in his front room.

Meanwhile, Maurice scrabbled desperately about the multi-buttoned electronic device, trying to use his limited knowledge of English to decipher which bit did what.

Frantically slapping at random rubber circles on the plastic control panel in front of him, the pictures on the screen became more garish and overexposed one minute, then monochromatic and muted in rapidly fading darkness the next. The animated images were replaced by flicking pages of text menus, whilst the underlying sounds of the television programme remained, blaring seemingly ever louder, as if in indignant protestation at their rude interruption, ensuring that obstruction from view, behind the newly static, word-filled screen, did not allow their presence there to be forgotten.

Unfortunately for him, even if he'd had all the time in the world to work it out, the majority of the buttons, and certainly the ones that he needed, were labelled with symbols rather than words. A small triangle, in either direction, for example, indicated volume up or down. Maurice took a last desperately hopeful guess and pressed the end of the button which had an upward facing triangle - and the decibels increased.

As a thoroughly confused, still half asleep Tom burst into the room, he was faced with an image which would remain etched firmly, forever in his memory; a mouse, sitting in his favourite seat, remote-control unit apparently to hand, as it always was when he himself sat there, watching the television, blaring out in front of him, a Tom and Jerry cartoon playing out on the screen.

Maurice turned and looked deep into Tom's eyes for a second time, caught in the act once again. There was a moment of fleeting recognition at the absolute absurdity of the situation before Maurice leapt from the cushion, onto the floor, and darted under the sofa, across the open expanse of kitchen floor to the space beside the washing machine, safe once more. As he huddled there, behind the worktops, ears ringing, heart thumping, he heard the volume of the television turned down to a more socially acceptable, neighbour-friendly level. "I don't believe it" muttered Tom, talking to himself as people who live alone often do "I've only got me *another* mouse!" and with that, he strode purposefully into the kitchen, opening the cupboard door under the sink. After a little rooting around, he took out a black, plastic tube. Opening an overhead cupboard next, he rearranged a few tins and jars, before finding what it was that he was searching for. "This should do the trick again!" he said to himself, taking out the packet of mini-battenbergs ....

The End (?)

Post-hu-mouse

No animals were harmed in the writing of this book

Praise for Maurice:

'Charming, intelligent, gently witty .... meanderings give rich detail as the story goes on and provide a vivid landscape. Honestly ... it is just lovely' – Isabella Rossi (and she's a teacher so she should know)

'It made me feel all warm and cosy. I was reading it in bed and making myself slow down so that I didn't finish it too quickly' – Carolann Merrells

'I read it in one evening. Started when I got home from work and only stopped for something to eat until I'd finished it. Captures the inner child in you and you can relate to the characters' – Suzanne House (Erin?)

'I love it. I don't see it as a children's book at all' – David Wills

'I read it with my daughter and we both love it' – Suzie Towse

'I started reading it when I sat for my niece last night and finished it today. Couldn't put it down. A powerful story that many will relate to – I definitely did. It caught me by surprise really as I found myself laughing out loud and had a tear in my eye' – Jonathan Parsons

'A scrumptious, heart-warming book which, once started, I could not put down. I was immediately charmed by Maurice and turned each page with eager anticipation to see where his adventures would take him to next. A truly alluring read, pitched perfectly for adults and children alike' – Elaine Wardrop

'You can tell that the author has been well educated' – Janet Forey (the author's completely impartial mother)

'Quite possibly the greatest book ever written. Much better than that Harry Potter!' – Anonymous

Got something to say about this book? Want to share your thoughts with the author? Feel free to get in touch at:

martinforey@tiscali.co.uk

Lightning Source UK Ltd.
Milton Keynes UK
UKOW040831250912

199573UK00001B/19/P